Unleaving, originally published in 1976, takes its title (as did the earlier book, *Goldengrove*) from lines by Gerard Manley Hopkins – *Margaret, are you grieving/Over Goldengrove unleaving?* – in his poem 'Spring and Fall'. Both books are set in a house in Cornwall much loved by the children who visit it, and the author has revealed that this was her grandmother's house in St Ives, where, as a young child evacuated from the dangers of war-time London, she was intensely happy. What she did not realize, until after she had written *Goldengrove*, was that Virginia Woolf had also lived in St Ives and had also looked out at the bay and its lighthouse. So the echoes of Virginia Woolf's writing reviewers found in both books seem to have their origins in the powerful influence of a particular place. *Unleaving* won the Boston Globe-Horn Book Award when it was published in the USA.

Jill Paton Walsh was born in London in 1937, and was educated at a convent and St Anne's College, Oxford. After her marriage in 1961, and the birth of her first child, she began to write as an escape 'from the boredom of being trapped in a small house with a baby that could not yet talk'. Her first book, *Hengest's Tale*, a historical novel, was published in 1966: her subsequent books have each been different, as she developed her literary gifts in different ways. She won the Whitbread Award for *The Emperor's Winding Sheet* (1974) and the Universe fiction prize for *A Parcel of Patterns* (1983).

UNLEAVING

Jill Paton Walsh

THE BODLEY HEAD
LONDON SYDNEY
TORONTO

British Library Cataloguing
in Publication Data
Paton Walsh, Jill
Unleaving. —(Bodley bookshelf)
I. Title
823'.914 [F] PR6066.A84
ISBN 0–370–30629–5

Copyright © Jill Paton Walsh 1976
All rights reserved
Printed and bound in Finland for
The Bodley Head Ltd
9 Bow Street, London WC2E 7AL
by Werner Söderström Oy

First published by Macmillan London Ltd 1976
This edition first published by The Bodley Head Ltd 1985

For J. R. T.
in several ways

Not how the world is, is the mystical, but that it is.   – Wittgenstein

The house is full of voices, full of movements. Whichever room one is in, one can hear in other rooms the sounds of talk and coming and going. The windows are open to the sea, to the murmuring wash of the waves, and the salt tangy air. The front door stands wide, admitting a quadrilateral of sunlight onto the carpet, and small Beth, her fair head blazing white with day, runs in, and out again, seeing and not seeing the meticulously-illuminated Turkey pattern, the grandfather clock counting its way towards four, and Gran making her way downstairs for tea, holding the banister rail all the way, patient at her own slowness. Reaching the foot of the stairs she straightens her cardigan, and advances with careful steadiness towards the living-room door, hand outstretched for the brass doorknob. The hand has crooked finger-joints and three rings, and a fretwork of blue veins beneath the brown freckles.

There had been a journey. A night journey, in a train with prickly plush on the head-rests that had indented Madge's leaning cheek, a train with sweating windows obscuring the only thing to be seen – the occasional light nearer or farther away in the passing featureless dark. Madge was in uniform, and her nightclothes were in a sportsbag, for the trunks were all locked away in the school attic; there had only just been time to catch the night train when the telegram arrived.

So she has reached the change point – St Erth for St Ives – in a leached and pallor-struck darkness, with an hour to wait for the first train on the branch line. The darkness slowly leaks away, and instead there comes a grainy greyness, like an old photograph, that makes you frown when you look, in which you can see some distance, but nothing clearly, and more of the gleam on the polished railway line than of anything else. Madge is entirely alone on the platform. The train arrives, and is empty. She gets into it alone, and it leaves. Into the rising morning light.

There is colour in the land by the time it reaches Lelant. Watery pale colour, suffused with gold. Pale sands, pale sea, so glazed and shining with sloping light that it looks silken grey; under Carrack Gladden, and not a single footprint on the wide, wide open sands, only the white waves moving. The train runs into the station, up to the buffers, that final full stop. Madge struggles with the door, opens it, gets out. There is nobody waiting for the train; it will stand for an hour before it returns.

Madge has been all night without sleep; she is light-headed. She feels as insubstantial as the town, mistily present, hovering vaguely in the gentle dawn. The sea in the harbour is shallow, creeping softly, with little waves breaking at the last moment, in small hushed splashings, as though not to wake, as though to come tiptoe up to

8

the leaning boats, and quiet dew-sleeked quays. What do I feel? Madge thinks. Do I feel anything? I have come, that is all.

From the station to the beach, and her footprints on it first, lonely, winding along the waves' edge. She takes off her shoes. She comes up the path, through the back gate, into the garden – a bird is singing – and walks across the grass barefoot. There is a gossamer web laden with shining dew strung between the handles of the French windows. To enter she must break it. She stands still. And turning, looks out to sea. The dawn has triumphed. The sun has risen out of the blurry wisps of restraining cloud; the sea is blue, blue, and breaks loudly white, and Godrevy has come out of the misty margin of the sky, and stands on the horizon, black rock, white lighthouse, the endless burst of surf at the foot of the rock frozen by distance.

The house is utterly silent. The shutters are up, refusing the dawn. Madge looks at the spider seal upon the door. When Paul is here there is sometimes a little ribbon of paper from the edge of a sheet of stamps glued across a door to tell-tale it has been opened, and Amy, Gran's pretty maid, grumbles, scratching the scraps off the paint with her varnished finger-nail. Madge has so acute a sensation that she is not there – that, ghost-like, she must enter without trace – that the sparkling trap on the door-handle deters her. She reaches in her coat pocket for her door-key – she has had a key to Goldengrove some three years now – and walks round the house to the front door, away from the sea, and lets herself in.

The house is silent within, and dark. Madge puts down

her shoes and her bag, and hangs up her coat. Her naked feet, dew-wet, leave ghost footprints on the polished floor. She turns the cool brass doorknob, and goes into the darkened room beyond the living-room door.

Tea is set on a white cloth. Lavish tea. Round it sit Gran and her summer houseful – her daughter Harriet, suntanned and sun drowsy, and Tom, her son-in-law, full of holiday cheerfulness, and their three children: Peter, and Sarah, and Beth. And how old are they now? Gran wonders. I always need reminding. Peter is eight, by now, "So Sarah is six, and as clever as clever," she says, smiling at Sarah.

"Yes. Sarah thinks poems are *true*," says small Beth, the youngest, and the deep one.

"Here, child," says Gran to her upturned freckled face, under a bush of bleached pale hair. "Have *cream* on it."

"I've already got jam," says Beth, thoughtfully. "Quite a lot."

"Have cream as well," says Gran, extending towards the scone on the flowered plate a thickly-laden spoon. "You'll like it with jam, I daresay."

"I like it here!" says Beth. "I like your house, Gran." And all the adults laugh.

That house was always a good place. Mr Fielding wanted

it, wanted it for himself and his son, and is appalled when he learns how his mother has left it. "It's quite inappropriate," he tells the lawyer. "Not right at all. I had always assumed it would be mine and Paul's. She can't have thought what she was doing."

"This will was not made recently," says the lawyer. "It was made the day after the settlement of your divorce, that gave custody of the son to you, and the daughter to your wife. Your mother had plenty of time to reconsider it had she wished."

"But . . . it is most distressing. There ought to be something I can do."

"Take advice if you wish, sir," says the lawyer, shaking his head. "But merely to leave property to a grand-daughter instead of to a son is hardly grounds . . . ."

And Madge, to whom her father's distress is shocking and distasteful, says, "I don't want it. Let him have it."

"I advise you to say nothing of that kind, till *you* have taken advice, Miss Fielding," says the lawyer quietly.

"Then let Paul have it," says Madge. "If it's mine, surely I could give it to Paul."

"Thank you, Madge, but I'd rather share it than have it," says Paul.

"Quite so," says the lawyer, looking with ill-concealed chill at their father. "Surely some arrangement could be found . . . ."

"And what of money to maintain it?" Mr Fielding demands. He gestures towards Madge. "Her mother hasn't anything, and she gets nothing from me; and a place like this . . . ."

"There is some money with the house," says the lawyer. "Enough to maintain it if Miss Fielding wishes to keep rather than to sell it."

"And a residue to me, I suppose?"

"A substantial one. Perhaps you do not realise the extent of your mother's estate? Shall I read the rest of the will?"

Gran sits like a queen among the teacups, pouring the pale amber liquid from a pot into the little fluted flowery cups, and naming her family one by one as she passes the cups among them. The cream and jam has produced a brief deep silence among the children, their fingers sticky in spite of licking and surreptitious wiping on their shorts.

"Can we go back to the beach?" they are asking in a moment or two. "Oh, can we? Oh, please!"

"You've been there all day," says Harriet. "And all the grown-ups are tired of being there with you."

"*I'll* take them this time," says Gran, getting up from her chair, both hands down on the chair-arms to raise her.

"Oh, no, Ma-in-law," says Tom. "Not you. I'll go."

"Oh, Gran, yes Gran, oh, *Gran's* coming!" the children cry.

"I can manage," says Gran. "I had a rest this afternoon. I can get down the path if I take my time, you know. I'll be sensible and take them to the big beach instead of our own little one, and then perhaps, Tom love, you'll bring the car down to fetch me back by supper-time. It's the climb up, you know . . . but I can manage *down*."

And off she goes, through the French windows, with the children all around her, tugging her skirt and hands, shouting and leaping, through the garden, through the gate, down the path to the beach, to the sea. The oldest child, solemn Peter, is carting Gran's chair and her knitting. Their voices, as they descend the cliff path, fade; and left behind in the peace among the crumbs and jam and unwashed tea-cups – someone has licked the cream-spoon cloudy clean – the grown-ups smile and sigh.

I should come down more often! Gran thinks, as the beach opens wide, opens great space around her, and the waves run vaulting towards her, and climb on each other's backs, and leapfrog over the rocks in bursts of pearly foam, and her eyes travel out to sea, far away, beyond Godrevy, beyond the lighthouse on its dark cleft rock. She stumbles ankle-deep in slithering silken sand, and the wind runs fingers through her grey silk blouse, and bellies her cardigan behind her, and ruffles her hair; and, suddenly skittish, she skips and runs a few steps among her pack of hallooing and circling children, wheeling and crying round her like gulls, though Peter now solemnly tries to make the deck-chair stay up, and curses mildly but passionately as he nips his fingers.

Soon she is sitting down, and fumbling in her bag, not for her knitting, but for some sweets. "Don't tell," she says to them, as she hands out forbidden goodies. "Don't tell, and wash your teeth well tonight."

"It's treasure," says Sarah. "Treasure. I'll bury mine. Deep and secret."

"Why?" asks small Beth.

"I'm a pirate."

"So am I!"

"Let's bury it all."

Gran closes her eyes that are watering in all that wind. Their voices come to her.

"Bury it all in the ground forever."

"Food for worms!"

"That's not chocolate, silly –" Peter's voice – "that's dead people!"

"Ugh!"

"Better be food for worms than have worms for food."

"Oh, I don't know, though. You could always sick up worms for food, but once you're food for worms that's irrevocable."

"What does irrevocable mean, Peter?"

"It means you can't take it back. It's for ever."

"Well, my chocolate is pirate gold, and worms don't eat that."

"You'd better *tell* them it's gold, you know, Sarah, because it does look and smell awfully like chocolate, and they might make a terrible mistake."

"I'll come and bury you in a minute!"

"*Oliver Cromwell is buried and dead*," sings Peter, in a thin high voice, digging with his wooden spade, "*Heigh, ho, buried and dead!*"

Gran sits, eyes closed, looking out to sea.

There had been a funeral. A walking funeral, for it was a local custom to have it so. Six men wearing black standing at the door of Goldengrove, the Minister with his black book open in his hands, and a crowd of folk of all kinds.

"*Whether we live, we live unto the Lord,*" says the Minister, as the six bring the coffin out to him, the sun bright for a moment on the brass handles, and then muffled again in clouds. The wind lifts the ring of lilies off, and tosses it to the ground. Someone replaces it. "*Or whether we die, we die unto the Lord; whether we live, therefore, or die, we are the Lord's.*"

The coffin begins to move up the drive onto the road. Mr Fielding goes behind it, and his second wife beside him. And Madge and Paul, in new black clothes, come next. All the way down Tregenna Hill people join them. Anyone who had sold Gran tea or apples, leaves the shop to walk. Down the turns of the steep road, and the coffin sloping on the shoulders of the bearers as they pick their way carefully over the cobbles, shiny with moisture from the rain that stopped only an hour since. Where the road turns sharply above Pedn Olva Point, the Minister halts, perhaps to give a respite to the bearers. The harbour lies in view below them.

"*Therefore shall they receive the crown of royal dignity, and the diadem of beauty from the Lord's hand. . . .*" Madge, standing miserably in the drab crowd, lets her eyes travel down to the harbour full of grey, troubled water, and the deserted quays against which exploding towers of foam mount and fall. A black dog rushes to and fro, barking wildly at the leaping spray.

"In the eyes of the foolish they seemed to have died,
And their departure was accounted to be their hurt,
And their journeying away from us to be their ruin;
But they are in peace. . . ."

Suddenly an explosion cuts through the Minister's voice, a bang like a gunshot. The maroon leaves an arc of fire in the sky for a short second, launches a brief green star in the daylight sky. Smoke billows thickly round the doors of the lifeboat shed, and a red pennant glides up to the masthead on its roof. The coffin-bearers shift uneasily. The crowd of mourners look at them; a second maroon finds them all silent, waiting, even the prayer suspended. The second summons cannot be ignored. The bearers put up their hands to the coffin, raise it from their shoulders, and lower it to the ground. One of them – Jeremy the fisherman – looks round with a brief glance to the Minister, before all six break into a run, and clatter away down the street. The coffin lies on the sleek cobbles, with its flower wreath askew.

"Really!" mutters Mr Fielding, distressed, nearly uttering his outrage. But the Minister is not disconcerted.

"Well, my good people," he says. "You see how it is. Now who will come forward to help bring our sister on her way to her last rest?" There is a moment of confusion. A little group of men measure up to each other to match the height of their shoulders, and one brother borrows another's dark coat, and struggles into it. Gently the coffin is lifted again. The Minister resumes his reading. *"For even if in the sight of men they be punished, their hope is full of immortality . . .*" but all the mourners' eyes are on the harbour below them. The lifeboat in its trolley is being trundled out. It fills the waterside street, looms high above the group of men beside it. At a sinister slow speed it is towed along the quay, the spray-bursts clawing at its tall sides as it goes. The faint sound of the coxswain's distant shouting punctuates the Minister's voice. But the cortege is moving on now, past the viewpoint, and down the narrow street. They begin to sing, a river of voices, flowing,

> "*There is a land of pure delight,*
> *Where saints immortal reign,*
> *Infinite day excludes the night,*
> *And pleasures banish pain. . . .*"

Down they go to the foot of the hill, past the parish church, and along Fore Street towards the chapel, singing,

> "*There everlasting spring abides*
> *And never withering flowers . . .*"

while the wind, ripping through the narrow passages and courts between Fore Street and the harbour, ruffles and tears at the pages of the hymn books, and blows the sound of voices through the town in broken gusts.

> "*Death like a narrow sea divides*
> *This heavenly land from ours . . .*"

and at the end of Fore Street, where the path of the

mourners comes out upon the quay, all eyes are for the water, and the lifeboat can be seen, just rounding the end of Smeaton's Quay, and meeting, bows under, the white rage of the storm. It looks small, small, now it is in the water, and tossed like a cork float on the contemptuous strength of the sea. In a moment it is out of sight.

> "*But timorous mortals start and shrink*
> *To cross this narrow sea . . .*
> *And linger shivering on the brink*
> *And fear to launch away. . . .*"

Madge sings too. And could it be true, she thinks, could it possibly be only a journey to some other place? Of course not, not possibly. And yet, she asks herself, remembering the other morning, when she came up to the house alone, entered alone, very early, where is Gran now?

> "*Could we but climb where Moses stood,*"

the swelling voices assert all round her,

> "*And view the landscape o'er,*
> *Not Jordan's stream, nor Death's cold flood*
> *Should fright us from the shore!*"

The coffin is taken into the chapel, and prayed over. The congregation spills over into the street; some people whom Madge hardly knows are crying. ("Your mother had many friends among us," the Minister has said to

Mr Fielding, whose eyes are dry.)

Madge hardly hears the prayers. The close atmosphere of the little chapel oppresses her, makes her feel faint. In a while Paul takes her arm and leads her out. She sits down on the step and gasps the cold air like someone saved from drowning.

"Are you all right, Madge?" asks Paul, anxiously. She nods. A little group of women, detached from the others waiting in the street, stand down on the shore where they can watch for the lifeboat. In the full harbour the moored boats heave and toss on their ropes, and the waves break loudly through the sound of singing from within.

In a while the coffin is carried out again, and the procession moves on, over the shoulder of the hill, through narrow streets of fishermen's cottages, and out onto the further shore, where the green burying-ground slopes down to the Atlantic surf. There is a great amphitheatre of grassy hill, curving round from the Island with its little chapel atop it, to the dark rocks of Clodgy Point. A moon of golden sand lies between, at the foot of the slope. And onto this shore the great surf rolls and roars. Half a mile deep, the breaking waves come on, in a fury of whiteness, and, beyond, the sea stretches leaden-grey, ruffled and troubled as far as the eye can see, with the sky pressing low, rain-threatening, above it. The force of the wind strikes them, and the vastness of the sound of the surf. Not only the soft plosive ejaculations of the breaking waves, but beneath that, continuous, like a great engine, like a wild beast, a deep unceasing roar, the grinding of the sea bed – water on rock, element against element to eternity.

And the mourners pick their way down the path, between the gravestones – Church to the left, Chapel to the right – towards the twin chapels of rest, nestling close together, but still two, one for each kind. Safely sorted out, the dead lie waiting for a judgment, which can hardly, thinks Madge, make *that* distinction between them. She is expected, she discovers, to stand close by the earthy rim of the grave, to see the coffin into the ground; *"Earth to earth, ashes to ashes, dust to dust, in sure and certain hope of the resurrection to eternal life ..."*

Now it is nearly over. The crowd begins to sing again, in loud unison, pitting their voices into the teeth of the wind.

> *"Ah lovely appearance of death,*
> *What sight upon earth is so fair!*
> *Not all the gay pageants that breathe*
> *Can with a dead body compare ..."*

There is a sudden tremor through the crowd. And they all look out to sea, to see the lifeboat, barely visible in the storm-tossed water, making its way back, and just coming into view round Clodgy Point, dipping in and out of sight behind walls of grey salt water, but sending up high and clear the green flare turning white that means "All saved". Its mission is safely accomplished, and all is well. The singers do not hesitate or falter, but relief and joy sound in their voices triumphant as they steadily sing on:

> *"With solemn delight I survey*
> *The corpse when the spirit is fled*

In love with the beautiful clay
And longing to lie in its stead."

It is suddenly all too much for Madge, who runs away, down the green slope, dodging between the granite crosses and the coffin-shaped marble memorials, to leap over the wall at the foot of the churchyard, race across the Zennor road, and jump down onto the sands, to run along the seething margin of the sea. Faintly the singing pursues her:

> "*In love with the beautiful clay*
> *And longing to lie in its stead!*"

but she runs, fiercely, till the surf blots out all other sound, and leaping from rock to rock at the end of the sands, she climbs the Island to the top. Watching the bursts of foam at its jagged foot, with spiralling flights of nameless feeling she stands there, wind-lashed, and, soon, drenched in rain and spray, till she has seen the lifeboat safely in.

"I've come to take you home, Ma-in-law," says Tom. Gran starts a little as she hears him, for she was far away.

"Come on, kids!" he bellows, and, gathering up chair, knitting and old lady, he Pied Pipers with her along the beach, while a litter of children trail and scamper behind them. In a while the bath at Goldengrove will have a long shoal of sand lying in the bottom of it, and Harriet's goodnight story will be stopped less than half-way through, its audience all asleep.

There have been other deaths, other rescues. Only last year, Gran tells her family over the dinner-table, with an avalanche of wax cascading down the red candle in its silver candlestick, the lifeboat was called out in the depth of darkness, and the wind blowing fit to lift the tiles from the roof at Goldengrove. "When I hear the maroon," says Gran, "I can't sleep again till I know they are safe back in. That time they were gone a long while; in the morning I could see the lifeboat station doors still standing wide – you can see from here if you look, from the bedroom window. I went down after breakfast to ask, you know, and I met Mrs Nance, the coxswain's wife on the quay, waiting around, poor soul, and not looking as though she'd slept a wink all night, and the sea still making an uproar. When they came, almost mid-day – that's sixteen hours they had been out – they had four living and two dead aboard. Terrible. A terrible thing."

"You shouldn't be troubled by it, Mother," says Harriet. "You surely need your sleep. You have been very ill, and it isn't as if you could *do* anything."

"Well, no, Hal love. You're quite right I daresay, but I can't help the way I'm made. Then perhaps you're not so right. One can't do anything; is that a reason not to feel anything?"

"Well, most people manage it, Ma-in-law," says Tom, grinning at her.

"When I was a girl I knew a boatman quite well," says Gran, "who was lost at sea in a lifeboat accident. And you know, that man feared drowning, feared it greatly. I remember once he told me that he regretted having learned to swim. Most fishermen don't, he said, and it was better not, that drowning if it comes may be quick and easy. And you know, I so *admire* that; out they go, only when the weather has defeated some other souls, and, going, they risk for themselves what they save others from. So brave – like loving – and they make so little of it, take it so for granted."

There is a brief pause, then Harriet, changing the subject, says, "I meant to tell you, by the way, that twice this week I've seen someone hanging about the gate, looking into the garden."

"Oh? That sounds sinister, Hal. What sort of someone?"

"Not to worry, Mother; he wasn't wearing a dirty raincoat; he was a very respectable-looking, upright, elderly gent."

"Grey-haired and with an ebony cane?" says Tom. "I saw him too. He really must be lurking about."

"Well, next time anyone sees him," says Gran, "ask him in for tea, and we can find out *why* he's lurking."

"Don't be ridiculous, Mother," says Harriet. "You can't ask a total stranger in for tea. He might be a burglar."

"That's just what she would do, though," says Tom, vastly amused. "She'd ask a burglar to take tea, and interview him on why he was doing it. Can't you just see it?"

"*Would* I?" says Gran, delighted. "Well, perhaps I would. So next time anyone sees the burglar, just invite him in, and we'll see what I'll do."

"You're incorrigible, Mother," says Harriet. "And, no, dear, you can't have coffee, you know it keeps you awake."

"What with coffee and lifeboats, it's amazing you sleep at all," says Tom, still smiling.

"As far as *coffee* goes," says Gran thoughtfully, "it was Oxford that ruined my character. Definitely. It's a very immoral place. I'll have a little brandy, then, please, since *you* are all drinking; why should I be left out? The lifeboats, I suppose, are from further back still."

"I really believe, Ma-in-law," says Tom, "that nobody gets as skinless as you except by being born that way."

"Oh, no," says Gran. "We're all born fairly coarse and cheerful, *I* think; it's life that flays us."

"Coarse and cheerful certainly would describe our lot," says Harriet.

A thin, high-pitched wail sounds eerily from the landing. "Sarah dreaming again," says Gran. "I'm on my way up. I'll see to her and forego my brandy. You two enjoy your coffee in peace."

One would not think of Oxford as a place where characters are ruined, to judge by the earnestness with which Miss Higgins wants her pupils to go there. Madge only expresses a little uncertainty about it, and she is summoned to the Headmistress's study, ostensibly to talk about entrance exams, and which colleges Madge is to try for.

"Correct me if I'm wrong, Margaret," Miss Higgins says, "but do you not own a house now, a house by the sea? In Cornwall, I seem to remember?"

"Yes," says Madge. "Goldengrove. I inherited it."

"I will tell you why I ask. I have a friend who needs a house to rent for this summer. Is it a large house?"

"Yes. But I don't let it," Madge says.

"He is a university professor, Margaret, from Oxford. An old friend of mine. He wants to take a reading party of undergraduates. I thought an acquaintance with some studious people might be of use to you, my dear. Will you be there yourself, do you think?"

"No," says Madge. "When it was Gran's we went there a lot; but now it's mine we can't. It's all shut up and there's nobody to run it, and my mother won't let me be down there by myself."

"Cornwall is very pleasant. Doesn't your mother sometimes go with you?"

"You know how my family quarrelled," says Madge. "It's my father's mother's house. My mother won't set foot in it. She wants me to sell it – 'cash it in', as she calls it."

"Well, how would it be if Mr Jones and his wife opened it up and ran it for their students, and paid you rent for it, and you went down there too? Might not that work out rather well? I will speak to your mother, if I may."

So Goldengrove is unlocked and opened up for Mrs Jones, who walks round it, liking it, with lists in her hands, and asks Madge before she opens the linen cupboard for sheets, or uses the china. Madge helps all she can, but cannot imagine the house as full of people as Mrs Jones intends, and is awestruck by the college servant in his shirt-sleeves, unpacking books, and is overwhelmed by suddenly missing Gran, and Gran's way in this house, and Gran's small kindnesses. And though she isn't anywhere, Madge mourns (for where could she possibly be?), here above all is where she isn't. Here reminds me. Madge goes down to Laity's on the quay to buy coffee in incredible quantities, and on her return takes refuge in the attic sunroom, lying on the wide cushioned window-seat, her nose pressed against the window, watching the cars drive up to the front door, and the strangers arrive.

There are, of course, a lot of young men. They arrive in twos and threes, carrying holdalls and bulging sportsbags. Madge loses count – six? eight? Here are two more – a short stocky dark-haired lad, and a very good-looking tall fair one. That must be eight of them. Now here is a taxi from the station and three small children, and a grown-up man in a shirt and flannels. Mrs Jones is emerging through the front door to kiss first him, and then them; that must be Mr Jones and three Jones children. Madge can see little more than the tops of their heads from up here. It strikes her suddenly that perhaps she ought to be downstairs to welcome them. After all, this is her house. Even though she isn't in charge . . . . She jumps up, and starts down the stairs, two at a time.

Swinging herself rapidly round the banister post on the landing she collides with someone coming up – the dark boy, with the fair one. She almost knocks him over.

"Hullo!" he says, smiling. There is a pause. She waits for them to make way for her, but they hesitate.

"I'm Madge Fielding," she says.

"Oh," says the dark boy blankly. "Oh – er, I'm Matthew Brown, and this is Andrew Henderson."

"How do you do?" says Andrew Henderson.

"Yes," says Madge. "Well, I was going downstairs..."

"Of course," says Andrew Henderson, standing aside.

Another car draws up as Madge reaches the entrance hall. She watches a thin, very tired-looking woman in a suede coat get out of it, followed by a striking man with dark hair, grey at the temples, and then by a small thickset child with a shock of red hair. They seem, Madge thinks, rather old to have such a young child. They come leading it by the hand.

"This is Professor and Mrs Tregeagle," says Mrs Jones at the front door, offering a welcoming cheek to the other woman.

"You must be Madge Fielding," says Mrs Tregeagle. "This is Molly. Say hullo, Molly."

Madge stoops towards the child, hands held out, and smiling. "Hullo, Molly," she says.

The child looks up. Its face is very ruddy, with almond-shaped pale blue eyes, and hardly any lashes. It smiles, and as it does so the smile fills with spittle, which overflows, and oozes down its chin. The eyes swim inwards into a squint.

Madge sickens for an instant, then realises, then covers up and steadies her smile. Forcing herself, she bends and picks up the child, staggered at its solidity and weight.

"Would you like to look at the view?" she asks it. "You can see the sea from the other side of the house."

"See, see," says the child. And then, as Madge moves out into the drive to carry it round through the garden, she sees someone watching her. A boy has got out of the car on the other side, a grown boy, Madge's own age, or a little older. He is lean and dark, with a long nose and full lips. He must be the Tregeagles' son, with his father's face, and his mother's curls, but what Madge notices first is the stare he is giving her – looking at her, she thinks, astonished, with an expression full of anger – but the moment she catches his eye he turns away, and stalks into the house. Flinching, she takes the child onto the lawn, and plays with her there, with elaborate kindness. The child is pleased. It plays a lumpish dance with Madge, and chuckles a lot. Together they pick a bunch of flowers from the untidy borders, and go in to find a jam-jar for them.

"Where will you want to sleep, Madge?" asks Mrs Jones, meeting them in the hall. "How good of you to cope with Molly."

"There's an attic I like a lot," says Madge. "I'll have that, I think."

"Attics, too? How many? Could I put some of the young men up there? Oh, I'll come and see in a minute when I've just seen to this." And she pins up on a board in the hall a typed list of *House Rules* which begins *Breakfast, seven to eight. Silence for individual study will be maintained throughout the house till one o'clock.*

Upstairs, Madge unpacks her own books. "Looks as

though I'll have time for these after all," she thinks. And Mrs Jones finds what used to be Amy's room, next to Madge's sloping attic with its view to the sea, towards Godrevy, and decides to put Patrick Tregeagle there.

Toiling up the stairs to the very top, taking her time, taking time to draw her breath, Gran reaches at last Sarah's bedside in the little whitewashed room with its sloping ceiling.

"What's the matter, Sarah?" she asks. "Did we hear you call out?"

"I had a bad dream. Gone now."

"Sure, are you? Tell me, if telling helps," says Gran, sitting heavily on the bed, and taking the child's damp hand.

"I was falling, for ever and ever," says Sarah, shuddering. "But I'm all right now, Gran."

A dream of falling. Patrick. Madge is moving round her attic, sitting in the window, looking out to sea, to the lighthouse. A storm wind is blowing, although the day is bright. The water is opaque and sullen, the surface dark like hammered metal, though between the cloud-shadows on the bay the sun green-glosses the top inch or two, and the waves break white all over it like huge snowflakes, and glaciers of foam fill the rock crevices of Porthminster

Point, and avalanche over and over the black rock-crags below her.

Madge thinks about the boy with angry eyes whom she can hear moving about in the next room. He can't be much older than me, she thinks, and he looks interesting, and if he weren't angry it would be a good thing to gang up with him, to have some friend-and-ally among all these strangers – why ever did I say they could come? – till Paul gets here next week. Perhaps if I show him the way out to the roof valleys he'd like that.

She knocks on the attic door. He does not answer properly, just grunts. Madge marches in, before her courage fails her.

"I've come to show you this," she says, and opens a little door in the wooden panelled wall under the slope of the eaves, which gives into the dusty space over the joists, facing a dirty window. Madge stoops through the door, pushes the window open, and wriggles out. The roof is made of slate hills and valleys, all zig-zag up and down, with lead gutters in the bottoms of all the dips. For a moment or two Madge is alone, walking unsteadily in the narrow gutter, and then the dark boy comes too. They lean against a slope of slate and look at the sky. "I want to see over," he says in a while.

"You can climb up and sit astride the ridge if you're *very* careful," says Madge. He begins a scramble up. But when he reaches the top the wind buffets him, rolls him nearly over, whips his hair into his eyes, and tugs at his shirt, filling it like a white sail.

"Help!" he cries, and hastily dismounts the ridge, and

slides down into the sheltered lee of the roof-valley where he lies askew, legs up one slope, back leaning on the other, and begins to laugh.

"Are you going to show the Jones kids this?" he asks.

"Oh, no!" says Madge. "And don't you dare. This is a secret, Paul's and mine. It's only you I told."

There is another pause. The sun has warmed the tiles out of the wind to almost tropical heat. They lie snug like lizards.

"Who's Paul?" he asks in a while.

"My brother. He's coming next week."

"So why are you here? I'm here because I always have to come, wherever they go for their beastly vacation parties. Mother and Father I mean."

"This is my house," says Madge.

"Wow! You don't care much about cracked slates, for a landlady."

"Well, I'm not into that yet. Perhaps I'll have to. What a horrid thought. Hey, if you're always on these reading parties, you can tell me what it's going to be like."

"Bloody boring. Very quiet mornings, when you get skinned for making a noise, while they all read, and they won't let me play; then brisk walks and debates in the afternoon, and then they read papers to each other some evenings. I go out if it's not raining, and lie as low as I can if it is."

"What did you mean, they won't let you play? Aren't you a bit old . . ."

"The piano."

"Oh," says Madge, blushing, but Patrick is smiling.

31

"Come to the beach," says Madge.

"The one I saw from up there?"

"No, that's one of the big ones. We have a small one all our own. Well, you can't own a beach, really, but there's one you can only get down to from the bottom of our garden. I'll show you."

So down. Through the window, squeezing, Madge first, across the dusty patch of joist and plaster, and through the door to Patrick's room, with its huge dormer window facing over dark wind-tossed trees to the south. "What was this room for?" asks Patrick. "It's a sunroom; Gran had a couch here to lie on and catch the winter sun," says Madge, hurtling down the poky panelled stairs to the landing with bedroom doors, down the main stairs, racing through the hall and the porch with its mosaic tiled floor – "Who was W.H.B.?" says Patrick, looking at the monogram in the lozenge in the middle of the tiled design – round the house at a run, leaping down the steep descent of the terraced garden, out of the back gate to the cliff path, where the view arrests them for a moment – beach, town, harbour, quay, rock, sea, the green hill of the Island rising behind the harbour, and beyond it, right over it, far, far, the immense wide deep blue sea, across the skyline to the lighthouse – but only a moment, then down the stony zig-zag path, running, Patrick ahead now, swinging round the turns and corners in the hairpin path, over the railway bridge, and then sharp right, off the sedate and ordinary path, past PRIVATE LAND, the way nearly overgrown from either side by nettles and wild flowers, out onto the point, and down, down, to the golden shore, on which the loud waves roll, leaping in great toppling glassy walls, one behind another, hissing and jumping, exploding in soft furies of foam, casting scallops of spume-webbed water over the shining wet slopes of sand, and pulling back in looped ropes of froth-edged, puckering shallows, over which the next wave breaks and sweeps, and the two of them run, swerving up and down the slopes of sand, flirting with the water, down as it retreats, and, Help!, racing away as it gathers strength to fling its pawing edge after them, engulfing their running feet. Wet to the knees and laughing, they slow up, walk on.

"This is a North-Easterly," Madge says to Patrick. "It turns the town inside out; this is usually the sheltered shore, and the far one the wild one."

A great wave breaks, and charges up the beach in bolsters of thick foam so that they skip hastily out of its way; and as it retreats it leaves a little brown bottle at Madge's feet. She picks it up. The sea comes back again, pawing the sand, reaching for her.

"No message," says Madge, looking at the bottle. She hurls it high and far, as hard as she can, out into the staircase of rising breaking water, and they walk on.

"What will they be like, all those clever people?" Madge wonders aloud.

"They're not so clever, really. Only about *the subject*. About people, they seem rather stupid to me, usually," says Patrick.

"I knew a professor once," says Madge. "He was blind."

"Quite."

"No, but he was *really*," says Madge protesting. "Is your professor father very famous? Might I have heard of him?"

"Shouldn't think so."

"Only I thought I'd heard your name before, somewhere."

They have walked some fifty yards farther when the waves, breaking in front of them, roll the brown bottle up the beach at dizzy speed, and deposit it again at Madge's feet.

"Heavens!" says Madge, picking it up. "It wants me to have it!" But once it is in her hand the sea churns and rages at her, pours into her shoes, and worries round her ankles. She stands there, looking at the bottle, and then at the sea, unsure.

"What if it had a message in it now?" says Patrick.

Madge shudders at the thought. "I'll throw it back," she says, "but if it comes again we'll *know* the sea means me to have it."

The bottle leaves her hand in flight, and describes a long arc out of the turmoil of the surf. They walk on, right to the end of the little beach, and turn back, retracing their steps. Madge thinks about the bottle. It will not come back again; the sea has a direction; they were walking with it, now they are going against it. But she has forgotten the eddying backwash where the surf is thrown back off the rock point. In a short while they can see the bottle again, bobbing and rolling in the edge of the boiling surf a little way ahead of them – hurtling inland on a burst of breaking wave, and then dancing out again in the back-

34

wash. In silence they stand and watch it. To and fro it goes. Madge does not wade after it, but merely waits, and by and by the bottle is laid on a stretch of glossy, momentarily dry sand within reach. She stoops, and possesses it. It lies cold in her hand while she looks with astonishment at the cavortings of the sea. And the sea tosses in the wide bay, girds the lighthouse with a changeless brief wreath of white, and towers and falls before her with the same mock ferocity as before.

"I knew at once you were an unusual person," says Patrick behind her. "Or nearly at once, because Molly liked you. I've forgiven you that first moment, you know, because she liked you later."

Turning to look at him, Madge finds his eyes intensely meeting hers. They are as brown as the bottle in her hand.

"What an odd thing to say," she says. "You are a strange one, Patrick Tregeagle."

"What about you, then?" he says. "What about a person who gets presents from the sea?"

"Hey, look!" says Madge, laughing, holding her bottle high. "The sea gave me a present! It really did!"

"Oh, I'll beware of you!" says Patrick.

It's a Cornish name, Madge thinks, still wondering later in the day where she had heard it before. And that thought reminds her. She goes into the little room, the "front parlour" that served as a library. The two dons have assembled all the students there, and they are in deep

35

discussion. Unabashed, Madge starts to search for a book. It takes her a while to find it; Gran's books have all been moved into one corner. Instead, there are volumes bound in heavy fake leather, with a college crest on the spines, and unfamiliar titles. What strange things philosophy books are called! *Leviathan*; *A Critique of Pure Reason*; *Action, Emotion, and Will*; *A Discourse on Method*. Method for doing what? And why isn't there one called *Thinking*? And here is one called *The Blue and Brown Books*. It is just one book, bound in the same deep green as all the others. Madge moves along the shelves, looking for *Cornish Folklore*, and as she does, gradually begins to listen to the conversation in the room.

". . . a whole constellation of topics to bring to your attention, concerning the soul, the connection between soul and body, and, reluctantly, since it has occupied the minds of so many philosophers, immortality . . ."

"Pre-existence, surely, is of equal importance . . ." It is the fair-haired Andrew Henderson speaking up.

"It can't be of equal importance, can it?" says Madge, amused. "Because it's too late to do anything about it, whereas if we're immortal we shall have to prepare to meet our doom."

Nobody answers her; nobody even looks at her. There is a pause. Then Professor Tregeagle says, "Yes, Andrew, that seems a logical pair. As I said, we have to probe a constellation of inter-related topics . . . ." And as if repeating himself reminds him that he has been interrupted, he frowns for a moment.

Madge finds *Cornish Folklore* and flees the room.

"You're just not used to it, that's all," says Patrick, when she tells him about it. He has found the piano at the far end of the dining-room, and is trying it out. "Nobody interrupts them. I wouldn't; neither would either of their wives. Listening with due humility is allowed – contributing is not." He strikes four solemn chords in sequence.

Matthew Brown arrives, seemingly looking for Madge. He pushes back the dark tuft of hair that falls over his forehead, ineffectively, and grins at Madge.

"Don't take offence, will you?" he says. "None was meant."

"Oh," says Madge. "Was what I said very stupid?"

"Not stupid – just not philosophical."

"Non-philosophical remarks, for the enlightenment of our young friend," says Patrick, from the piano, "are the class of all remarks made by non-philosophers. Or, in plain English, if you are not studying philosophy what you say doesn't count."

"What if what you say is so reasonable that it jolly well does count?" asks Madge.

"It *can't* count," says Patrick. "If you aren't a philosopher you are always offside."

"Take no notice, Miss Fielding," says Matthew. "Professor Tregeagle is a brilliant man. If he doesn't always notice social niceties . . ."

"This is Patrick Tregeagle," says Madge hastily, through another set of mocking heavy chords from the piano.

"Oh," says Matthew, "I *see*. Well, whoever he is, his father is brilliant, and I admire him."

37

"And rude with it, whenever his mind is elsewhere," says Patrick. Matthew shrugs. "I tried," his eyes signal to Madge, and off he goes. Madge takes her book upstairs.

She finds it at once – here it is –TREGEAGLE. There are dozens of stories about him. Alive he was the wickedest man in Cornwall; dead he is a wild and evil spirit. *His is the voice that howls in the storm over the moorland heights, and keeps the villagers awake. To master him he must be bound to some hopeless task – to emptying Dozmary Pool with a cockleshell drilled with a hole; to weaving ropes of sand along the restless tides' edge*. Well, if he was a man once, I suppose he can have descendants, thinks Madge. I wonder if Patrick knows about it? He won't find out from me, that I do know. And till supper she reads in the book the stories her Gran used to read to her, years back – tales of the Knockers in the mines, and the Spriggans in the heather, and the sad Lady with the Lantern, crossing the churchyard wall, and looking all night among the wave-washed rocks for her shipwrecked child.

The train from St Erth is a sleek diesel slug, two carriages long, rattling under the drop below the garden, snaking round into the station among the parked cars. Harriet is holding Beth up to the window in Gran's bedroom to see the train come. There is too much to look at, sea and beach and town and harbour and hill, and the child has to be talked to attention.

"Cousin Emily is coming to see us," Harriet says. "You remember her. You liked her last summer."

"See the boat," says Beth, pointing out to sea.

"Look, here comes the train," says Harriet. "With Emily on it. You remember Em."

"That big girl with a hole in her trousers," say Beth.

Below them, Em jumps out of the train, dragging a battered canvas satchel, wearing torn blue jeans, her long hair swinging to her waist. A dark sweater is tied round her waist, sleeves knotted against her navel, the rest hanging like a tabard over her backside.

"There she is!" cries Harriet.

"Oh, good, good. So she caught the train," says Gran from her afternoon lie-down on the bed behind them. "One never knows with Em."

"Em! Em!" shrieks Beth. "She's going to the beach. Isn't she going to come and say hullo?"

"Along the beach is the quickest way here from the station," says Gran. Em weaves a path along the edge of the waves towards them. "There seems to be somebody with her," says Harriet. For a lean black-clad figure has detached itself from the crowd disembarking from the train, and is following Em along the beach, two steps behind her. Em finds something in the sea-wrack at the waves' edge, and shows it to her companion, her outstretched arm linking the two tiny figures in Harriet's telescopic view.

"No message," says Em, and throws the bottle back. The two figures run diagonally across the sand, and jump the little stream and come nearer, but out of sight, up the zig-zag path to the house.

"Did you invite some friend to come with her?" says Harriet.

"No, dear, but . . ."

"We haven't a room ready. Where can we put another person?"

"They can share, or something, Hal."

"It seems to be a boy, Mother," says Harriet.

"Where has Em gone?" demands Beth. "Isn't she saying hullo?"

"He'll have to go in the attic then," says Gran. "There's room. There's always room here."

"This is Jim," says Em, putting her scruffy bag down in the hall. Jim is wearing jeans and a black sweater. His hair is long, hanging in a tousled mass to his shoulders. He is tall and thin, and were it not for the owl-like gold-rimmed spectacles he wears would look like a walk-on part in a cowboy film.

"Hi," he says, shaking hands with Gran, and smiling down at her from head and shoulders above her.

"This is Jim, Aunt," says Em to Harriet.

"Yes," says Harriet. "We weren't expecting anyone with you, Emily."

"There's room . . ." says Gran. "Let me look at you, Em love. Have you grown at all? Grown different, I see. I don't know about taller."

"Don't worry about me," says Jim. "I've got a sleeping bag. I'll kip down anywhere."

"We can clear one of the attics," says Harriet. "It's just that we weren't expecting you."

"Now, don't *fuss*, Hal dear," says Gran. "I expect you two would like a cup of tea after your long journey?"

"Yes, if it's going," says Jim. "Look, what about that summerhouse thing on the garden wall at the foot of the garden? That looks great; can I sleep there?"

"Heavens!" says Harriet. "Won't it be damp and cold?"

"It'll be fine," says Jim. He smiles at Harriet. "And I won't be in the way there. O.K.?"

"Well, if you're sure you'll be all right..." says Harriet, dubiously.

The tea is served on the terrace, on little cane tables among the deck-chairs. The adults sip it, and pass the biscuits. Neither Em nor Jim come to drink theirs. But the garden below the terrace is riotous. Em and Sarah and Beth are in flight round and round the house, through the shrubs, along the paths, bent double at a run, fleeing and hiding, and Jim and Peter are roaring after them, howling and leaping in ambush, and the children become hysterical with excitement, their screams and laughter becoming indistinguishable. When the noise finally persuades Tom to rise from his chair to see what is going on, there is a heaving mass of bodies, all flailing arms and legs, on the lawn, from which he presently makes out that everybody is sitting on Jim. "Ugh! Arrgh! Mercy!" cries Jim.

"Seems an amiable brute, anyway," says Tom.

"I rather think," says Gran, "that Jim is the one her father approves of."

"He looks like a navvy, or a plumber's mate," grumbles

Harriet. "And obviously lives like a tramp. Fancy wanting to sleep in the belvedere."

"He may *look* like a tramp," says Gran, smiling mischievously, "but I think he's an undergraduate."

"People get degrees in plumbing, these days, I expect," says Tom.

"Yes, dear, but not at Balliol," says Gran. And it must be middle age that makes people so sticky, she thinks smugly, for *old* age leaves *me* all right. It has escaped her notice entirely that if an attic had needed clearing out this hot afternoon, it would have been Harriet who would have had to do it.

Em appears on the terrace like a pantomime entrance, leaping the lavender hedge, and landing neatly between two chairs. "Can we take this mob down to the beach till supper?" she asks.

"Oh, do. Certainly," says Harriet, relenting a little.

"I don't think I'd have spent hours playing with kids when *I* was an undergraduate," says Tom.

On the beach time drifts, suspended in the heat. The undergraduates are all up in the house, reading of the last days of Socrates. Down on the sands of Porthminster beach – "The children prefer it, and you can get ice-cream," Mrs Jones has said in response to Madge's offer to show her the special one — are Mrs Jones and Mrs Tregeagle, sitting side by side in deck-chairs for which by and by the chair-man will come and take their sixpences, with a huge striped beach-bag between them, full of towels and coffee in a thermos, and buns, and lavender oil to repel insects – I'm not surprised it does that, thinks Madge, sniffing – and paperback Agatha Christies, and Mrs Jones's knitting, and wooden spoons for the children to use as spades. "Safer and cheaper," Mrs Jones says. The youngest of the three Jones children is digging a castle nearby. Molly, too, is digging with a spoon, though to no purpose, achieving neither mound nor pit in the patient silting surface of the warm dry sand.

Patrick lies face down, stretched out on his bathing towel, propping arms on his elbows, and chin in his hands. Beads of salt water gleam on his back, drying off in the sun. He looks vaguely out to sea. And Madge sits beside him in a white dress, under a huge straw hat, with a book on her knee. The page glares dazzling white at her, unreadably bright, and she is sleepy with sun and lunch. They had been talking earlier; now they are silent.

The sea is smooth and tranquil. The waves are so small and late they hardly look real. Rising from the sun-shot shallows like little jade lions they arch green, glossy backs, come rearing and pawing a little way, and break foaming, tossing their suddenly tawny manes. Behind them in the glass-clear green water lie shimmering golden nets of floating light. In the distance Godrevy light, haze-softened, looks like a stick of blackboard chalk against the sky, and the sea lies quiet all the way there, like the waters of some limitless lake.

Molly finds a shell, a crab's claw, and shows it to her mother, tugging her skirt. Mrs Tregeagle shoos her gently.

"Go and play with the others, Molly," she says. Patrick stiffens, and turns his head to watch. Molly staggers towards the little Jones boy, playing nearest. His castle has battlements now, and windows made of pressed-on mussel shells. He stands up as she comes, and gets between her and it, arms stretched wide to stop her. "You walk on my castle and I'll hit you!" he says. "You *get*, or you'll be sorry."

Molly trots down the beach towards the others. They are whirling at the run round the scribbled paths they have drawn. Molly begins to run, too, treading on all the lines, and blurring them. She laughs her low-pitched chuckle. Soon she is circling alone; the others have withdrawn without a word spoken, have left their spiralling mazes to her trampling naked feet, and migrated yards along the beach to the edge of the stream. It is a little stream of fresh water, disgorged onto the sand by a rusty pipe through a grill; where it falls it has cut a whirlpool that bubbles thick with sand. Overflowing from that, it runs down into the sea, making channels and shallows and meanders, cutting little gorges and rapids like a geography lesson. The two Jones girls begin to dam its flow. Molly wheels drunkenly on, alone. Soon she sits down alone, and looks at the sea.

The two women are talking about college houses. One will be available when old Grimbly retires; there will be a shuffle and change about.

"I'd like the one in Walton Street," says Mrs Jones. "But we'll never get it. Not unless Hugh is made Dean. But the college doesn't really appreciate him. Perhaps if

44

he became Dean, though, we could do better than Walton Street."

"We couldn't have Walton Street. We need a garden. And a fence. A high one. Molly can climb these days." And here is Molly again, returning to tug at her mother's skirts.

"Oh, do go and play!" says Mrs Tregeagle, sharply. Molly starts off towards the stream. And Patrick lies still tense, watching, with Madge beside him. He is watching so intently that Madge, still serene and sleepy, and lulled by looking into vast lovely distances, watches too. They see Molly's dumpy figure in the distance, reaching the dam-builders. They see the two girls, bent over their labours, and digging frantically, straighten for a moment as she comes, and face her. Then she turns round, and comes away, retreating.

Patrick gets up, and strides down the beach towards her. He takes her hand, and leads her back to them. And Madge jumps up too, and follows, sure he is making a mistake, and yet not quite wanting to call out to him, not wanting to speak, just to catch his eye, and glance, "Be careful; are you sure?"

A big pool of water is building up behind the sand dam. It brims it, sneaks round the ends till choked off with another pile of sand. It licks at and topples the crests of the sandy battlements. Patrick leads Molly by the hand right up to the bank of the pool. "Surely she could help?" he asks, and so catches, full-face, the expression of revulsion which crosses the pretty, knowing countenance of Prudence Jones, flecked with sandy splashes from her struggle with the pent-up stream. Her sister avoids looking; simply flushes and turns away. They all stand frozen for a moment; and the meek and tiny stream has built up enough ferocity at its confinement to overbrim the barrier, and scour through it with joyous speed. The defeated engineers gaze at Patrick with sullen reproach. He turns on his heel, and marches back to the deck-chairs, still leading Molly by the hand.

"*Don't* send her to play with them, Mother!" he says.

"Why ever not?" says Mrs Tregeagle in a pained voice, and Mrs Jones says at the same time, "Oh, no! Were they unkind?" And Patrick says, choking and furious, "You know why!" and suddenly races away from them down the beach, plunging into the sea, and swimming, head down, arms flailing, boring his way out far, beyond the diving raft, and on and on, as though to reach the horizon.

He leaves trouble behind him. Mrs Jones stands up and yells, calling her offending offspring to her.

"Why won't you play with Molly?" she demands, as they come within earshot of a normal voice.

"It's not *that*, Mummy," says Prudence, aggrieved. "She really ought not to come there, that's all. That whirlpool is awfully deep, and it sucks down. It's dangerous."

"Oh," says Mrs Jones, disconcerted.

"You really ought to stop her coming after us," says Prudence gleefully, as they start back to their abandoned project.

"Come and play with me, Molly," says Madge.

It seems to get hotter and hotter. The sea looks almost

oily in the glare. Molly wants to pick up shells, and hand them to Madge, and take them back again, over and over, grunting a bit, and digging her soles in the sand. She will not play burying feet, or making castles, or any variation Madge contrives. Mildly amused at first, and then gradually stupefied with boredom, Madge sits, taking shells, and giving them back again. After some long while Patrick comes striding up the beach, leaving a trail of disclets of wet sand from his dripping body, and comes past without a word, stooping to pick up his towel without stopping, and races towards the path for home.

And in a while longer Molly, handing her shells over ever more slowly, falls asleep, and Mrs Tregeagle moves her deck-chair to cast some shadow on her sleeping child, and Mrs Jones gathers up her three, and begins a lucky dip plunge into the beach-bag to hand out tea. The sand on her fingers sticks to Madge's sugar bun, and grinds against her teeth. She isn't hungry. She slips away and goes in search of Patrick.

The house is quiet and cool. Madge brings sand with her on her feet and clothes; it is alien here, out of its element, suddenly gritty and uncomfortable. The fresh open-air salt smell of it mingles oddly with the smell of polish and warm dust, and the hot open-window scent of drifting heat off the garden, that fills the indoors. Madge climbs to Patrick's room, and taps on his door. He does not answer. She waits. After a while he pads softly barefoot across the room and opens the door.

"Are you all right?" Madge asks, feeling foolish, not knowing quite what to say.

47

"What will become of her?" Patrick says.

"Or of you," says Madge, "if you are going to feel like that about it."

"It doesn't matter about me!" says Patrick in his choking voice. And then, "Oh God!" and he plunges down the stairs out of sight, still barefoot, and disappears into the garden.

Hours later, when dinner is laid, and he still has not returned, Madge finds him in the summerhouse, sitting in a ruined chair, gazing at Godrevy, far out, and coaxes him to come in.

Propped into an angle of the hillside, with a cushion for her back, Gran feels for a moment like a parcel – put down and not forgotten, to be picked up later with relief that no harm has come. In front of her the grass slopes easily to an edge, and disappears. And the party has scattered, diverging like ships on different errands. Only the voices, unrelated climb back to her: the cries of children discovering small wonders. Until a face appears over the little rise to her right, then shoulders, arms, bare midriff, shorts, bare legs. Sarah, a scurry of flashing legs, rushing towards her, as if she had no time at all – not a moment to spare. It is age that has no time, thinks Gran, and age that takes it, all the same.

What brings her? A crisis? An accident? A small foot too near the perilous high edge – leaning over, looking down? Of course not.

"Can I have a biscuit to be going on with?" Sarah calls. "The ones in silver paper?"

Gran draws the hamper towards her. Harriet probably wouldn't allow it, with proper tea-time so near, she thinks, but Harriet is some little way off, and the endless conspiracy between young and old is in force. She gropes in the basket, hands out a biscuit. "Here," and, silently, she pushes another one after it.

"Oh, *thanks*, Gran!" says Sarah, but the words are left behind, thrown over her shoulder, for she has run away from them. Gran smiles, remembering in her legs the feel of scurry. And in a moment Sarah is back, to add her afterthought: "Can I have one for Peter as well? Can I have two for him? Or shall we have one-and-a-half each?"

"What about Beth?" Gran says. "Take two for her." And really, she thinks, I like it here. Hot grass, high above the sea, and a fine prospect all round, back across the bay, or out to sea. I like it in spite. . . . The cliffs are a grand sight, one would have to admit, although so far to fall. And who could not like the little wet clouds of froth, floating salt-spray spume, like cuckoo-spit flying, blown from so far below on the smart off-shore breeze? She sees her son-in-law stand on the brink to take a photograph, and smiles. It will be like a poster for a railway holiday, she thinks, all bright blue and dark rock, and melodramatic, with precipice and wave. He could get a postcard; the focus would be sharper and all for sixpence. Now if he faced about . . . but her mind refuses to turn, refuses with eye or mind's eye to contemplate the lighthouse from here, from this different angle, and eerily near. Though she

49

knows how it lies, dark against the sun on its sloping island in a sea that glitters with floating but unextinguished stars of light; how it looms, peering over the top of the cliff with its one Cyclops eye. She deliberately fixes her eyes on the smooth grass, the clumps of thrift, and the little gold bird's-foot trefoil at her feet, and deliberately drowses away in the heat, like some sailor, giving Godrevy a wide berth, sailing by.

If Miss Higgins thought highly of the company of intellectual people, Madge reflects, then surely she, Madge, is supposed to find glory in it. Glory of some kind . . . inspiration? . . insight? Or is she perhaps to learn from them, share their perception, gain understanding? But perhaps Miss Higgins herself has never been on a reading party. For the reading party does not seem very inspiring to Madge. Only one of the eight young men seems what Madge imagines an intellectual to be, when off duty. He is given to striding up and down, talking to himself under his breath when not actually reading. But the others are more interested in climbing. The porch is cluttered with their gear – coils of rope, and little pickaxes, and rows of pins in canvas belts, and heavy boots with studded soles. They talk eagerly about this face and that face, and use words Madge doesn't know. They are all rather suntanned and beefy, and always very brisk and cheerful; except for the mutterer, who is called Jake, and for Matthew Brown, whose opinion of rock-climbing is given in three words: "Not for me."

And so all morning the house is breathless with their need for silence; Patrick runs his fingers silently over the keys of the piano, and looks at the clock; Madge reads the volumes of Yeats and D. H. Lawrence that Miss Higgins recommended, and learns the splendid bits of poems by heart. The younger children are on the beach, whether they will or no – not that they show the least sign of tiring of it.

At lunch there is cheerful talk to listen to, but it is all about who is walking where and who is climbing what. Andrew Henderson, Madge notices, will never make up a group, always goes off by himself, even if he is climbing very near some of the others.

"Why don't you go with the others, Andrew?" she asks him once, meeting him in the garden.

"I prefer to climb alone," he says.

"Isn't it scary, all alone?"

"Oh, no," he says. "One can concentrate better. One has only oneself to worry about."

"Oh."

"It's not only that; you can stop when you feel like it. Nobody looking to think you are being a bit cautious, or that they could manage that, even if you can't. You don't have to push your luck."

Madge finds all this very interesting, but it isn't exactly intellectual.

The nearest distance to the intellect Madge can come is sitting listening to them talking in the evening. They occupy the comfortable end of the living-room, and read

and discuss round the hearth. And Madge does not understand the discussions at all, and yet in an odd way is ab-
sorbed by them. They seem to soar at once into a realm
so abstract that it *has* to be both beautiful and profound,
Madge thinks, rather as one thinks that the stratosphere
has to be clean. The alto-cirrus clouds shine above us, and
we see their shapes, she thinks, but we do not feel the
wind that moves them. I can see the *shape* of this talk – a
ferocious capacity for doubt, a search for precision as
heroic and unnecessary as all the rock-climbing, a surgical
capacity for laying bare the bones of things. Bones are
narrow, hard and dry. And, God! how fuzzy I am. It has
never occurred to me to doubt that the I that thinks is the
I that I am, for instance. And bemused, she begins to pick
up and dip into the books that lie round the house, looking
for a foothold, for a little light. *An Essay Concerning
Human Understanding* she finds, and, opening at random, reads:

OF THE REALITY OF KNOWLEDGE: *I doubt not but my
reader, by this time, may be apt to think that I have been
all this while only building a castle in the air, and be ready
to say to me: to what purpose all this stir? Knowledge, say
you, is only the perception of the agreement or disagree-
ment of our own ideas; but who knows what those ideas
may be? Is there anything so extravagant as the imagina-
tions of men's brains? Where is the head that has no
chimeras in it? It is no matter how things are; so a man
observe but the agreement of his own ideas, and talk
conformably, it is all truth, all certainty. Such castles in
the air will be as strongholds of truth as the demonstra-*

*tions of Euclid. That a Harpy is not a Centaur is by this
way as certain knowledge, and as much a truth, as that a
square is not a circle.*

Madge reads. Why does this make me remember the
attic? she wonders. What am I seeing? She is seeing Paul,
in her mind's eye, sitting beside her on the bed in the
attic room, very small and neatly made, in grey-and-white-
striped pyjamas, and a book, someone reading from a
book:

> *They told me you had been to her*
> *And mentioned me to him;*
> *They gave me a good character*
> *But said I could not swim ...*

and you think, Madge realises, light suddenly dawning,
you *keep* thinking, that if you concentrate only a little bit
harder, only a little bit longer, or hear it once through
again, you will understand it; but however long you try
the moment eludes you. I remember now, Gran reading
Alice to us when we were small, and how Paul lit up and
laughed. And yet, of course, it isn't quite the same, not
really, for soon one realised the trick, knew that there
wasn't anything there to get a grip on ... but with this
stuff. ... She closes the book and turns it to read the
spine. *John Locke:* I've heard of him. So I suppose if I *do*
try harder .... I must improve my mind, it clearly isn't
good enough. I must make myself good. But not yet; not
now; right now I shall go for a walk.

The reading party are all spread out on rugs and warm stones on the top of Zennor Hill, by Zennor Quoit. The young men have walked here, all the way along the cliff path, but the dons and wives and children have come by car, carting food and rugs and thermos flasks. The hilltop is laden with geological debris; grey stones stacked up like toppling piles of oat-cakes, or littered everywhere in lichen-splotched lumps. One of these piles is the Quoit – made on purpose, and with a hollow chamber inside, to be a burying place – but no one seems quite sure which. The eroding wind has played such improbable tricks here that it is hard to argue that this or that could only have been made by human hands; for human hands, when they made one of these stone stacks, whichever one, were content to ape the brutish untidyness of the geological process. The stones are all grown round by gorse and heather and upland grasses, and humming with insects. The Jones children are playing hide-and-seek in among the outcrops; Molly is still steadily eating. Mrs Jones and Mrs Tregeagle lie stretched in the sun. Madge and Patrick lie face down on a tall flat rock, looking down on everyone. They are overlooking the edge of the world.

West of them, shadowy against the light, are the last heights before Land's End; between lie a few farms, a scatter of patchwork fields, bathed in soft heat-haze sunlight, with a cloud shadow crossing here and there. And the land plateau ends, abruptly, and beyond are the plains of the sea. Raising one shoulder into view is the dark rocky bulk of Gurnard's Head. No more of the cliff can be seen, nor the remorseless, pawing, sapping assault of the sea on the foot of the landwall; only a tranquil blue shimmer melting into the sky. Midway to the floating edge of the land lies Zennor, its church tower squared clearly with sun and shade, its few houses clustered round it, and a ribbon of road winding by.

Whatever Patrick may find to hold his attention in all this, it is the conversation below that engages Madge. They are talking about innate ideas. At first she is adrift, through not knowing properly what "innate" means. But gradually her limping understanding picks up a thread or two. They are saying – or are they only saying that other men have thought it? – that there might be inward knowledge, inhering in the soul. Perhaps before anything was learned by us, there were things we knew, that all men know. Are there some truths so crystalline that they compel the assent of any human soul? Or does the soul bring into the shades of life some small reflected fragments of the bright light of some other place, trailing a few clouds of glory, though it only be to know that a thing cannot both be and not be at the same time?

The young man with the cropped red hair thinks that it is not any particular proposition, or set of propositions, of which there might be innate knowledge, but it might be rather a knowledge of the laws underlying propositions, a sort of subconscious early-warning system for detecting invalidity. Madge imagines that; one might know, not exactly where the wood will split, but that there is a grain in the universe, and which way it runs. And, ah, she thinks, how marvellous such knowledge would be – *I want it!* How does one get it?

They are saying, now, that if God exists, then the innate could be his mark upon the soul, the potter's fingerprint. Is there perhaps innate knowledge of God?

"But could innate knowledge then be lost?" asks Matthew Brown, in his flat northern accent. For no knowledge of God has ever appeared to *him*. There is something wrong with this remark, for it does not impress the others as clever, as it does Madge. They find it both expected, she sees, coming from him, and unsubtle.

"Were we to *accept* that there is innate knowledge," says Mr Jones, "we should have to tackle Locke's refutation."

"Which is," says Professor Tregeagle, "that no idea alleged to be innate, even the simplest, does in fact command universal assent." Behind him the bobbing golden heads of the children dip and bounce between the sunlit stones. "For it is evident that children and idiots have not the least apprehension or thought of them."

Madge stares at Molly, whose coarse features and sluggish understanding are thus enough to strip the soul of God's fingerprints, extinguish the undeniable truth, and send us into the world naked with all to learn. Molly has gathered a handful of stones, and is putting them at random on top of the nearest boulder.

"I'm off. Coming?" says Patrick, on his feet abruptly beside Madge.

They pelt down the long slope, and trot along the road to the village. Zennor Church is quiet and cool inside. Madge finds the Merrymaid carved on a pew end, and tells Patrick the tale she heard long ago from Jeremy.

"Don't you go singing so sweetly out by the skerries, young Madge," Jeremy had said to her, grinning. "Or the Merrymaid'll come and get you to sing below the waves."

"He was called Matthew Trewhella, the boy the merfolk stole," Madge tells Patrick. "They could hear his voice, from where they swam, when he sang on Sundays, in Zennor Church. And it seemed mortal hard to them that earth folk should sing so sweetly, and all of them be dumb. And for years after they took him, folk could hear his voice in Pendour Cove, as he sang to her who took him." And what would it sound like, she wondered, a song from beneath the mute and roaring water? Just a note or two, pure and simple, she thinks, something very plain, like a scrap of knowledge, coming with a new soul from some clearer atmosphere above.

"Look at this, Madge," Patrick is saying. There is a gravestone with a curious figure on it. *Of pagan appearance*, says the guide leaflet in Patrick's hand. *Possibly holding a serpent swallowing its tail—a symbol of eternity.*

And nearby another stone declares:

> *Hope, despair, false joy and trouble,*
> *Are those four winds which daily toss this bubble.*
> *His breath's a vapour, and his life's a span,*
> *'Tis glorious misery to be born a man.*

"I don't see what's misery about it," says Madge. And, "I don't see what's glorious about it," says Patrick in the same breath.

The heat is tremendous. There is no wind, and scarcely even a movement on the air. The garden is suffocating with sweetness as the fragrant oils of leaf and flower exude an odour which hangs over the wilting plants. The beach is like a desert, blinding, and too hot to walk on with bare feet, and even the sea has been stupefied into a glassy swoon, with languid waves rising wearily and sighing on the shore. The children are indoors, upstairs, drowsing naked on top of the bedcovers, in rooms with the curtains drawn, the attempt at a morning on the beach having sapped and defeated them. Downstairs the adults sprawl and sip tea. Tom is reading the *St Ives Times* – last week's copy, but he hasn't noticed that.

"God, how frightful!" he says suddenly.

"What?" asks Harriet, looking up from writing her postcards.

"Some child went missing from a picnic party on Zennor Hill," he says. "They think it fell down a mineshaft. Just listen to this: *The whole area is pitted with disused shafts. During the nineteenth century there were regulations that on abandoned mines all shafts should be made secure. In many cases a round collar of stonewalling was built, in others a simple fence, or timber platform placed over the mouth of the shaft had to suffice. During the passage of time some of these constructions have required replacement, but this has not always been done. Overgrown with brambles and hidden from sight, the occasional shaft remains – and the long drop into total darkness below. If this is what has befallen the missing child, there is little chance of finding or recovering the body . . . .*"

"How horrible!" says Harriet. Tom turns a page, and reads on.

On Zennor Hill the reading party's picnic is being gathered up to carry home.

"I can't think why the loaves and fishes redounds such credit on the Messiah," says Mrs Jones. "There always *is* far more left over after a meal than the meal itself consisted of. Now a picnic with *fewer* than seven baskets to pick up afterwards would be a much nicer miracle." Patrick and Madge can be seen below, climbing back to join them on the hilltop.

It is suddenly realised that Molly is nowhere to be seen.

They call, and begin to look for her, casually at first, then gradually more and more urgently, further and further afield. Andrew Henderson suddenly takes command, divides the terrain roughly between this line of sight and that, and divides also the members of the party, giving each a sector to pace over. A grim self-possession descends on everyone, as the task begins. The blithe unawareness of Patrick, still some distance off and perfectly at ease, infuriates his mother, who screams frantically at him, trying to pitch her terror across half a mile of sunlit gorse and stone.

"Listen, everyone!" calls Andrew, self-appointed captain, standing on a stone, and cupping his hands round his mouth. "Take *care*! There are some disused mineshafts on this hill, that may not be fenced!" It is as if he sees the shadow of his warning only after it is spoken. He goes pale. The long drop into total darkness gapes in everyone's mind. "I don't want to have to climb down one of those for *anybody*," he mutters.

But soon, before Patrick and Madge have approached far enough to distinguish the cries of Mrs Tregeagle, there is a shout nearby. Someone has found Molly asleep between one warm rock-slab and another, and Professor Tregeagle is running, stooping, picking her up in his arms, and carrying her towards her mother. Molly wakes at his unfamiliar clasp, and tries to give him the ghost of a flower which her strong grasp has taken, root and all, together with a random handful of grasses and prickles that were growing by.

"Present," she says, smiling. "Present."

At once a sense of foolishness sweeps over everyone. How melodramatic they have all been! They remember that things hardly ever really *happen;* misfortune is almost always just shadow-boxing. Or at any rate, that things hardly ever happen to oneself, or anyone one knows. And cool sensible young Andrew, who kept his head with Mrs Tregeagle going frantic at his side, and knew how to arrange a proper search, unfairly feels most foolish of all.

"What's up?" says Patrick, arriving.

"Nothing," says Mrs Tregeagle, hugging Molly. "Nothing. False alarm."

"Is that for me, Molly?" asks Patrick, taking the crumpled flower.

"*Nobody* has eyes in the back of their heads. Nobody could watch all the time," murmurs Professor Tregeagle, taking his wife's hand. "But it would help," he goes on loudly, "if Patrick pulled his weight, instead of going off like that. Does it always have to be your mother, Patrick, who keeps an eye on your sister?"

Only Madge sees the set of Patrick's face. He offers no reply.

Someone is playing the piano in the drawing-room. It is an elaborate, extraordinarily precise and patterned sound. It draws Madge from the garden, through the French windows, to sit in the window-seat at the quiet end of the room, and listen. The two armchairs either side of the bowl of dried flowers in the empty hearth are occupied by Professor Tregeagle and Mr Jones. It is the muttering Jake who is playing. His music is very domineering, despite its tact. It marches in on you, and orders your soul, undertakes a metaphysical spring-cleaning, in which every disordered over-emphasis is set to rights. It does not deny emotion, but it gives every shade of feeling only its true weight exactly, and no more. Madge surrenders to it, and savours a mathematical tranquillity.

After a while Jake stops, and closes the varnished lid upon the keys.

"Won't you go on?" asks Professor Tregeagle. "I, for my sins, have a son who not only prefers piano-playing to thought, but also Chopin to Bach."

"I have a letter to write before dinner, sir," says the young man, retreating.

"They're a very tame lot, really," says Mr Jones, sighing. "Not a patch on last year's." They seem not to have noticed Madge, who is put thus in the position of eavesdropper. But it's my house, she thinks rebelliously, and stays where she is, knees tucked up to her chin, sitting on the chintz cushion between the window-curtains.

"Perhaps we could strike a spark or two with a pop-subject. An 'if God' debate. The argument from design. That's quite fun to shoot holes in."

"Have we the patience for it?"

"Well, some bit of old-fashioned metaphysics to jolly them up . . . ."

"God, it's hot," says Professor Tregeagle. "You know, Hugh, quite a lot of the time I wish she were dead. All the time. It seems the only way out for any of us. Have you *seen* an adult mongol? Or the kind of home we could put her in when she gets too much for us?"

"My dear Gilbert, I'm sorry. I didn't realise how this afternoon's brouhaha had upset you. Let me pour you a whisky, and leave the debating topic to me. I'll think of something. Tell me – isn't she unlikely to reach adult life?"

"Maybe. They often are sickly. One almost wants it. And yet, for all that, when I thought something *had* happened to her . . ."

"Of course, of course. Drink up, Gilbert, you need it."

Madge, withdrawing, wanders in the heavy warmth of

the evening down the sloping garden with its spectacular view of sand and town and sea. She finds Patrick sitting in the hot shade of the summerhouse with Molly, trotting about grunting to herself, and dark-haired Matthew.

"We were wondering if we'd go and swim this evening," says Patrick.

"Or at crack of dawn tomorrow," says Matthew. "Will you come too?"

"Oh, yes, if you go tomorrow. But tonight I think I'll listen to the philosophy debate. It's going to be 'if God? or the argument from design'."

"Please yourself," says Patrick. "*I'm* not going to sit there listening to them in their cultured precise tones discussing obscenities!"

"God is hardly an obscenity," says Matthew, smiling.

"No?" says Patrick. "If the universe is designed, then God; if God, then the universe is designed. If God, then things are *deliberate*. Someone looked at my mother, and decided to inflict Molly upon her. Someone made Molly . . ."

"Me," says Molly. "Me."

". . . purposely with no capacity for growth and little for happiness, and chose us for her kin. There are, of course – I don't lose all sense of proportion – a thousand worse outrages occurring every day. How about senility, for instance? Now *there's* a funny practical joke to play upon a feeling creature! If God, he's a bloody bastard!"

"Patrick, no!" murmurs Madge, horrified.

"Ah, but there's the world to come," says Matthew brightly. "Our sense of injustice is caused by our partial knowledge. But in the light of eternity justice will be done; rewards in the hereafter await those who suffer now."

"And God is the great accountant, keeping the books? What kind of person could accept a credit in the hereafter in exchange for the suffering of some poor inoffensive creature now? And what are we to make of God's conduct which apparently consists of torturing people, and then paying them a reward providing their submission was abject? We know what to think of that, if it is perpetrated by a human being!"

"One could hardly give the God of the Bible much of a testimonial for good character, I agree," says Matthew. "But you'll have to admit the old boy can design tremendous sets." His eye travels over the shining bay below the summerhouse windows, over the green and gold further shore of sand-towan and pasture, and the white lighthouse on its black rock. "He's quite a conjuror; he does lay on a marvellous spectacle."

"And who are we to argue, you are about to say," says Patrick, sarcastically, "since we were not there when the foundations were laid, and all the stars of morning sang together. The argument from authority is a rotten argument, no matter who pushes it."

"Well," says Matthew, "where *were* you, Patrick my friend, when he shut up the sea with doors, when he made a cloud the garment thereof and wrapped it in a mist as in swaddling bands? Or when he said, 'Hitherto shalt thou come, and no further, and here shalt thou break thy swelling waves'? Have the gates of death been opened unto thee, and hast thou seen the darksome doors? Hast thou considered the breadth of the earth? Tell me, if thou knowest all things."

"But, Matthew," says Madge, outraged. "You don't believe all that; I heard you the other day saying you didn't believe in God!"

"No, I don't," says Matthew. "Though that isn't what you heard me say. Of course I don't. Like Patrick, I'd rather have random chance any day. But that's philosophy. It's like chess, Madge. If he plays the black pieces, I'll play the white."

Mrs Jones suddenly appears in the summerhouse door. "I've come to find you for dinner," she says. "You didn't hear the bell down here." As Patrick, picking up Molly, and carrying her, goes up the garden with Matthew, she says to Madge lightly, "Did I hear you lot talking philosophy too?"

"I don't *think* it was philosophy," says Madge. "It was important, and it wasn't cool."

"Goodness!" says Mrs Jones, suppressing a grin, and thinking: Just wait till I tell that to Hugh!

"Off you go, Emily love," says Gran. "Now there's a quiet moment, with the children all asleep. Jim will sit beside me and tell me all about himself." Emily saunters a little way, and sits on the lawn making daisy chains. Gran begins upon Jim. Shamelessly curious, she extracts from him the names and ages of his two brothers, a description of his father, another of his mother, and a third of his house, before she gets round to asking what he is studying.

P.P.E.? Does he like it? Do you need a grasp of maths to do the economics? What does he make of philosophy? . . . Emily, overhearing all she can, is half amused, half embarrassed.

"Yes, it is interesting, of course," Gran is saying. "It is fine as long as you don't take it seriously. Ethics particularly. Never take them seriously."

"That's wild advice, from a respectable . . ." Jim stops.

"From a respectable old lady to a nice young man," Gran finishes for him. "Don't take ethics seriously. Sounds bad, doesn't it?" She chuckles to herself. "Now Lawrence, D. H. Lawrence, was very against having sex in the head you know; it's the wrong place for it. I'm just as against having morality in the head. Tell me now, what do they think of Wittgenstein these days? Is he still Moses from the mountain? And what exactly does this Chomsky man mean by his something grammar?"

Jim's expositions go on so long that Emily, festooned with yards of daisy chain, gets tired of waiting, and eventually comes bounding up, saying, "Fancy you knowing anything about philosophy, Aunt!"

"Cheeky monkey!" says Gran, shaking her fist at Em. "Why shouldn't I?"

Madge sits, alone, at her high window, watching the

long ebb of the evening across the bay. She is thinking about Patrick. He is very puzzling, she tells herself, and then corrects the thought – (I must try not to be so foggy!) – what I mean is, I puzzle myself about him. He is like the sun coming out – he sharpens the edges of things, heightens the contrasts, light and dark. And I don't see why. Or do I mean I don't see how? I see some things it *isn't*. It isn't that he is handsome, for a start. Andrew Henderson is far better looking, with his fair hair, and wide forehead, and wide-set blue eyes. But Andrew is always somehow chill; one can like to look at him without liking him at all, as though he were a statue, or a picture of someone one doesn't know. He doesn't concern me at all. Looking at him is like seeing the departure time of a first class train that I'm never going to take anywhere. It tells me something I have no use for. But Patrick . . .

Patrick, she admits reluctantly, is almost ugly. Too long a nose; cheeks too lean; eyes set too deep. But at least I want to know. . . . He has weather in his face, endless changes. Like the sea below, he changes abruptly, varying wildly from one mood to another, and at worst ferocious, frightening. And I mind about it. Why should I care? Because I don't like him – she sees how true it is as she thinks it – I really don't like him much! He's too churned up; he makes too much fuss; he matters too much to himself. No, that's not quite it – everything matters too much to him. But then everything includes me – I feel I matter too. He pays such searchlight attention to one. He makes me feel what I say matters – the exact shades of meaning, the exact way I feel. Oh, dear, this doesn't look good, does it? It looks as if vanity is behind it, that's all. No, blast it, that's not it. After all, Matthew likes me too, and I hardly think about him at all. When Matthew is cheerful – well, Matthew always is cheerful; but when Patrick is, one is as pleased as at a fair-weather picnic, knowing how easily it might have been different . . . .

Darkness has engulfed the bay. There are stars to see, and the flash of Godrevy. Madge has fallen asleep where she sits, with the mystery of Patrick still unsolved. When a door banging wakes her, she rolls into bed still in her dressing-gown, and drowsily resumes her drift of thought. I can call him to mind so precisely when he isn't there, she muses; his long narrow hands, pale-palmed and sun-tanned on the backs, and the finger-nails cut off very square and short – for playing the piano I suppose. I can imagine him into a chair, and see exactly the angle he would sit in, and the set of his leaning head . . . and, damn Patrick, I shall go off by myself tomorrow . . . .

It is still hot. Madge is stretched out like a cat, on a warm corner of sand in the lee of a baking rock which keeps off the light breath of air from the sea. She swelters contentedly. The sound of the sea caresses her drowsing mind, pierced by gulls, crossed by the *chuff chuff* of a train arriving from St Erth. A golden brilliance transfuses her closed lids, and fills her eyes.

A shadow falls across her. She stirs; it remains. She

opens her eyes, shading them with her hand, and blinks up frowning at the young man standing over her. He is a black outline, aureoled in light. His gold hair blazes. He swings a rucksack off his back onto the sand beside her, and smiles. "Hullo, Sis," he says.

"Paul!" she cries, joyfully, struggling up to sit beside him, and lay a hot sunburned arm round his shoulders, over his damp shirt. "I'm so glad to see you! At last!"

"What do you mean, at last? I'm early."

"Yes, yes you are. Come and swim."

"Finding your clever crowd too much for you, are you, and wanting your own mugwump brother?"

"Well, they are a bit . . . ."

"A bit what?" He is laughing at her.

"A bit . . . . Oh, you'll see. Come and swim!"

"I'm straight off the train . . ."

"Your trunks must be in your bag, and I've got a towel. I'll buy you an ice-cream while you change."

The ocean may look hot; it looks, Paul says, like Green Chartreuse at the edges, it is so clear, and the shallows so lightened by the golden sandy floor beneath, and full of the endless web of floating wavering light. And it is sticky with salt, but it is always cool, even on the slope of the burning beach, and beyond knee-deep it is cold, sharply cold. It is, after all, the ocean, continuous from here to America, from here to the poles. It has its style to keep.

Hours later they trail up the path to the house, barefoot, swinging Paul's rucksack between them, and stop at the turn of the path to look at the view. They stand waist-deep in weeds and wild flowers just under the summerhouse, on the garden wall of Goldengrove, and through its open window they can hear voices: Patrick's, and Molly's.

"Here's a sweet for you, Moll," he is saying. "But first you must say something. Say for me, Cogito. Co-gi-to. Now you say it."

"Coggletoe," says Molly.

"Co-gi-to."

"Cogito," says Molly. Madge is obscurely uneasy. She calls to Patrick. "Hullo! What are you doing?"

Patrick's head appears in the open window. "This is Paul," says Madge. "He's my brother."

"I can see that," says Patrick, in a less than friendly tone. "Hullo."

"Hullo," says Paul.

"Whatever were you doing with Molly?"

"My father is under the impression that two-syllable words are her limit," he says. "I'm trying to teach her a word with three."

"But she *likes* words with three," says Madge. "She was saying petrol-pump and butterknife the other day, over and over. Try her on one of those."

"Petrolpump," says Molly, from behind Patrick.

"Say Cogito," he says, reaching in his pocket for another sweet and turning his back on his audience.

"Cogito. Sweetie?"

"Cogito ergo. Then sweetie."

"Why can't he try petrol-pump?" mutters Madge.

"*Cogito ergo sum*. It's a Latin tag. It means: *I think, therefore I am*," says Paul.

"Oh, *really*!" says Madge, in disgust.

70

"Cogito sweetie," says Molly cheerfully. It is obvious Patrick is in for a long session. Madge and Paul leave him, and go up through the house to the attics, where Paul is to have the room he always had, because Madge has saved it for him. The lunch bell goes in the depths of the house below them.

"Oh, damn that!" says Paul. "If they're all like that utter nutter in the summerhouse, I can do without meeting them all at once. Let's go down to the town, and buy a sandwich, and look for Jeremy to say hullo. Have you looked him up yet this time, Madge?"

"No," says Madge. "I haven't yet. I've been a bit tied up with . . . the utter nutter!" She suddenly laughs.

"Come on," says Paul. "Come out!"

Through Downlong, the district by the Island, through the maze of narrow streets and little cottages with steps up to the high front doors and pilchard cellars below them, past cottages set round little courts, they skip and laugh, looking for Jeremy. They find him at last, sitting in the sun in the lodge on the quay, by the sailors' chapel.

"Sold your boat?" says Paul, horrified at what he hears. "Sold it? What are you doing now?"

"Well, there weren't much in it, not now, you know, young Paul. A few trippers to take round the bay, or off to Seal Island. A string of mackerel to sell now and then. But not real work for a man. Mind you, 'ts our own fault. St Ives folk so dead set against Sunday fishing, so all the

East Coast boats brought their catches in to Newlyn. Trade's all gone there now, save for a bit at Hayle. I bought a little charabanc, that's what. I take people over to Land's End, or Kynance, or wherever. I'm doing all right. Tell you what, I'll take you anytime – we'll traipse off just like old times."

"You know, Jeremy," says Madge sighing, "you never took me to Godrevy, and now it's too late."

"Oh, I dunno about too late, then, girl," he says, smiling at her, his bronzed face crinkling deeply into a weatherworn pattern of smile and frown. "It's seldom that. Someone'll lend me a boat for that."

Paul and Madge wander all afternoon, from beach to beach, climbing the rocks, picking thrift at the edge of the grassy cliffs, talking. It is late when they climb back to the house, but, still reluctant to go in, they pass it, and go round as far as the Huer's house, where, long since, men watched for pilchards in the bay. Madge gazes at the endless show put on by the Almighty: the movement of clouds and waves in the soft evening light, the moon-shaped coves of sand, the black rocks, and white spume breaking on them, the panoramic sweep of the ceaselessly changing sea, a paper moon in a still-daylight sky. They sit there till the light goes off the waters below, and the golden eye of Godrevy begins its night-long winking to the count of ten. Then they come back through the shadowy bushes, and in through the gate to the garden. Through the open window of the house, music is pouring; the piano is storming through an outburst of passionate notes, raw feeling naked in the sound, like blood from a wound. The others have gone in to dinner, and Patrick is playing, alone, in a darkened room.

All afternoon the heat has thickened. The blazing sunlight has gone, and a low, grey sky like a thick blanket suffocates the day. Everyone is sticky and cross, and damp. Even Jim is sitting down, sharing the general lassitude. It sounds at first as if a light breath of wind is rustling the dry leaves – and then it begins to patter and drum; rain is falling, a heavy downrush of liquid darts under which the leaves tremble and bend; the earth dimples, the pavement makes tiny fountains. The adults leap up and run to close windows all over the house. Glazed with sliding streaks, the windows blur the leaves beyond, and distil a fresh green shimmer cleansed of distinct form. Gran, too, rises and goes, though slowly, to close the window of the living-room, and shut out the wet that is spotting the cushions and beading the painted sill.

So she is the first to see the children, her grandchildren, Peter and Sarah, and small Beth, dancing naked in the cool rain, their tender bodies shining wet with the falling drops, throwing their arms up, tilting their faces to the sky, eyes closed, mouths open, their bare feet drumming the soft wet grass, making a trodden ring among the daisies. They sway in sensuous abandonment under the rain god's soft palpation. Their golden heads are sleeked and darkened by the silver torrents, and become heavy, and shed bright droplets like the green leaves around them, the trees above them and the grass beneath.

Gran leaves the window unclosed. The adults gather behind her in the room full of stillness and stale heat, looking with a kind of awe. When Harriet speaks she does not say, "They will catch cold," but, softly, "They are not of our tribe." And Em and her Jim, who feel almost always the youngest, the strongest, closest to the rising sap, are upstaged entirely, and for a moment feel the sober steadiness of age.

But Gran looks and smiles, holding the window-catch and never dreaming of shutting the window. And in her mind the rain is an element of eternity, showing in its brilliant light-catching instant of fall the eternal aspect of the momentary now. Just let it catch the light in such a way, and the whole world shows this double aspect, an immortal brevity, an infinite particularity. It was Traherne – (will I never outlive quoting, and telling myself where the quotation comes from?) – who saw the orient and immortal wheat, which knew no seed and yet no harvest time. And boys and girls playing like moving jewels. *"I know not that they were born, or shall die,"* she murmurs. Coolness flows round her into the room, the rain softens, falters and stammers and dies away, leaving a pattering of laggard droplets sliding from sloping leaves and high branches, and falling late and reluctantly from the constellation of others on the diamonded leaf-webs of the trees. Gliding on leaf and petal, the drops collide and fuse into shining pools in the throats of flowers. The children circle slowly to a halt and sigh, begin to shiver, and hug their bare ribs with their thin glossy arms, and run indoors. The spell-bound adults move back from the window. And the warm wet ground of the garden gives off a smell of earth, a smell of the leaf-mould of summers and summers back, and of green growth now.

There are wet Man-Friday tracks all over the polished floor in the hall, and the towels are mud-streaked, and full of blades of grass. Small Beth is worried about what the grown-ups will say, and sits on the bathroom floor picking grass off Gran's towel for ages after the others have gone to play upstairs. Harriet finds her later, sleeping in the towel, curled up on the bathmat, the grass still sticking firmly to both towel and child.

"Not today, then, Madge girl," says Jeremy. He is sitting on the quay in the warm sun, with his shuttle in his hand, mending nets among the other fishermen. Madge has brought Patrick, too, for after all, it would be nicer if he and Paul would get on.

"Is it too rough?" asks Paul, looking at the sea. It is sportive today, leaping about, tossing and choppy, and the crests of the waves are wind-sharpened before they break, to a ripple-flaked edge like a flint blade from the museum. The sun strikes through the dark water and gives it a translucent blue-green glaze. Yet the weather is hot, and the wind on their faces light. "Surely the boats go out in worse weather far than this?"

"No," says Jeremy. "T'ain't too rough." He knots off his work, and nods to the net's owner before drawing them away out of earshot. "T'ain't rough," he says. "But we can see Ghost Island. The fish'll wait till tomorrow."

"It wasn't fishing we wanted," Patrick ventures, smiling hopefully at Jeremy. "It was a trip to Godrevy."

"I've even bought some fresh baked heavy-cake to give to the lighthouse men," says Madge.

"Bless you, there's nobody on it now," says Jeremy, shaking his head at the bag of sugar-coated raisin buns Madge holds out to show him. "The light went automatic years back. You'll have to eat your heavy-cake yourself, that's what."

"Oh," says Madge, sadly.

"What did you mean about the island, Jeremy?" asks Paul, and it's all right for him, thinks Madge crossly; he's been to Godrevy. Jeremy took him once when I wasn't there.

"You go up the hill, and look seawards, and you'll see 'un," says Jeremy. "Now if a poor seaman lands on a ghost island, it fades away with him on it, and he's never seen again."

"And is that why you won't go out today? Really, Jeremy?" Madge is entranced.

"Now does that seem like a rum idea to you, young Madge, or to your friend here?" Jeremy is smiling. "I'm glad to be off the sea. She's a fickle hoor, that's what. Any folk going on her in small craft know that. Know that mortal well. I've had a good run, never lost a boat, never been in the water head under. Time I came ashore, afore my luck changes. And when it comes to a little trip to oblige an old friend, well, I'm not running in the teeth of any rum ideas about luck; I'm not aiming to. Now t'ain't just me, see. None of the other men are out today. Boats all in harbour. Or young Tom Parsons – Josh's boy, you know. Last Good Friday he goes off with the other kids sailing model boats on Stannack Pond; and his won't sink, see. His dad knocked two or three holes in 'un, but the bugger stayed afloat. So they ain't bin out this season at all. Not once. You know whyfore? Because they used to reckon if the wicked old lady took your model she'd leave the real boat alone; that's why. T'ain't only me, Madge my love."

"Of course not, Jeremy. Another day will do," says Madge.

"Tell you what, though. I've got an errand to do up Zennor way this morning. You walk up over and meet me there, and I'll take you for a drive-round. Land's End maybe, and Sennen. What do you say to that?"

"Great," says Paul. "Thanks. We'd like that. Hey, Jeremy, though, your name's still up in the lifeboat shed, on the crew list, isn't it?"

"That's different," says Jeremy sharply. "Got to go then, haven't I?"

Leaving him, they climb the slopes of the green hill that is called the Island, slipping on the glossy grass, and stopping to feed each other with handfuls of hot currant-stuffed heavy-cake, and finally they reach the little chapel on top of it, and sit in a row of three, Madge in the middle, on the little wall that runs round it.

And they can see Ghost Island, quite clearly, out to sea, very far away, north-easterly, beyond Godrevy: a steep-sided lilac shadow, just perceptible in the misty shining distances between sea and sky.

"*I* think," says Paul in a while, "that's Lundy Island."

"Can't be, can it?" says Patrick. "The curvature of the earth would stop one seeing so far, no matter how clear the day."

Paul gets out his compass, and takes a bearing. "I'll look on a map when we get home, but I bet it is," he says. "What else could it be?"

"Well, it *could* be Ghost Island, lying in wait for poor seamen to land on it, all ready to spirit them away," says Patrick. "I can't see that that's any more unlikely than suddenly being able to see round the curve of the earth."

"You *are* a nutter!" Paul complains. "You're as bad as Madge!"

"Well, I don't mind being that," says Patrick, smiling.

Through the churchyard, above the roaring beach. In the tall dewy grass the gravestones stand knee-deep, declaring the names of the bodies, the faith of the souls. *She is not dead, but sleeping*, says this slab. *In sure and certain hope of the resurrection*, says another. *He has kept the best wine until now*, says THOMAS WEDGE, 1881 *to* 1925. *An unknown sailor, drowned on these shores* R.I.P. says a granite slab. For Gran there is only *And* MARY *his wife*, under the dates of long-forgotten Grandfather. But this place is radiant with the bright light of the shore, and loud with the sound of waves.

And beyond, across the road, out onto the grassy cliff-tops round the tall brink of the black rough broken cliffs goes the path to Zennor. It curves round, skirting the wide sands to Clodgy Point, all littered with rough chunks of stone, untidy with the detritus of ages. Here they climb a rock and sit, looking across to the Island from its unfamiliar western side, and, sideways, across the great surf rolling in. Between them and the Island the whole depth of the bay is white with breaking water. Roaring, the curling frothy crests sweep across to the sands, combing out behind them long tresses of undulant smooth white, their soft violence making an endless dim uproar on the shore. Beyond the Island, Godrevy rock seems to have moved inshore, and to lie close to the headland on the far side of the bay; beyond that, further and yet further headlands fade eastwards in shades of haze – indigo, lilac and violet. At their feet, fountains of foam rise and fall, leaping into view up the cliff-face and falling in shining showers of white beads back again.

"Why is it called heavy-cake," asks Patrick through the last crumbling sweet mouthful, "when it's quite light?"

"Ah. They upcountry folk don't know much, do they, Madge girl?" says Paul. Patrick puts up fists to him, and they shadow box.

"*Because*," says Madge, "it used to have pilchards in it. Like mince-pies used to have meat, actual meat."

"What do you mean, 'because'?" demands Patrick. "To say 'because' in a well-formed formula, you have to assign a reason for something. What kind of reason are pilchards?"

"Well...."

"Of course, they could have been *weighty* pilchards, I suppose – vast heavy creatures like small silver whales!"

"Fool!" says Madge, giggling. "You caught pilchards by having a 'hevva' – a kind of hue and cry after them – called from the clifftop by special look-out men, and they directed the boats rowing in the bay below them, to put a big net all round the shoal. First a hevva; then cooking heavy-cakes."

"Do you think they had currants in them as well as pilchards? asks Paul. "Because I don't know if I *could* have eaten that . . ."

"Don't know that I like pilchards *much* even without currants," says Patrick.

"Well, Cornishmen like them. Gran's maid, Amy, said her mother used to cook them in a pie for all her brothers, with the heads all sticking up through the pie crust," Madge tells him. "And do you know what they called that?"

"Tell me. I'm no good at guessing," says Patrick.

"Starry-gazy Pie!" cry the other two in unison, laughing.

They walk on. Town and bay now lie all behind them, and they clamber on the rocky clifftop, looking down spout-holes through which the wild sea cannons upwards and dews them with light drifts of spray. It is salt on their lips. Madge finds a spectacular crag to sit on, while the boys scramble off somewhere. The sun warms her back, and on her face the spray drifts, floating landwards across the grassy brow of the rock-walls, and shot with brief faint rainbows where it catches the sun. She watches, dream-bound and rapt. Suddenly something falls across her head, and casts a shadow-web across her view of spray; she starts, and finds herself tangled in a length of torn fishing net which Patrick has found and, creeping up behind her, has thrown over her, and is holding down.

"Caught you!" he says.

"Oh, I say!" cries Paul, from a rock nearby. "You ought to throw the tiddlers back, you know. It's not sporting to keep them!"

"Grr! Agh!" yells Madge in mock fury, writhing about in the net.

"Ah, but I don't fish for sport, you see," says Patrick. "I fish for survival. And I've got her tangled."

"Well, you'll have to untangle her just for now, if we're getting to Zennor in time," says Paul. "Come on."

And Madge really is caught up in the net, her struggles having thrust legs and arms through the rents in the mesh, so that it does take Patrick's help to disengage her.

"I'll let you go, Merrymaid," he says. "But you'll promise me not to jump back into the sea."

"I'll promise that," she says, smiling. "But I'll not make any other promises, mind. I'm not good for fishes with gold in their bellies, or three wishes, or magical calm in terrible storms. I've nothing of that sort to give."

"Haven't you, though?" says Patrick, as Madge runs after Paul.

It is too hot to run far. Between the outcrops of rock the grass on the clifftop is bright, rippling with a wind-silken sheen in the sea-breeze. And it is patched yellow

81

with bird's-foot trefoil and clumped with tufts of sea-pink. And high. It has a hilltop wide-open feeling, and the view is of the glittering and dark blue sea, and it feels wider and nearer than on a beach, in spite of the beach's fuss and fury of rolling surf. The land here does not slope, or crumble away, or give the sea space and licence to come in and out, but stands out boldly into deep water, and offers an unyielding confrontation to the endless turmoil below.

Jeremy is parked beside the church. His bus is hot with standing in the sunlight but when they get moving the flow of air through the wound-down windows soothes the stickiness of their skins. Madge puts her arm out, and claws a handful of onrushing air, and holds it pressed on her palm. Her hair blows wildly. The road winds and ribbons round the hillsides, under the barren tops with their heather and gorse and stones. Westwards and westwards they go, past the tall engine houses of abandoned mines, with their towering chimneys, their squalid grandeur, outlines black against the sun, gaping windows, sloping roofless eaves. The road leaves the coast, turns right, and at last runs out to the very end of the land. With everything behind them, they get out of the bus. There is an asphalt car-park, and an ugly hotel. There is a kiosk selling postcards, and lumps of polished serpentine made into vulgar souvenirs, and ice-creams. A strong wind blows off the sea. Climbing over the car-park wall the four of them walk the brink path, looking westwards.

They can see the land ending with craggy magnificence. A huge humped rocky height, nearly as tall as the land itself, stands islanded in the sea below; across the silver-streaked, twinkling plains of the sea are more rocks, and a lighthouse standing on them.

"There's men still on that one, Madge," says Jeremy. "You were crestfallen that Godrevy's gone automatic, I saw that. Well, cast your mind out yonder. There's the Longships light; that's got men on. And look southward now. No, that way. Can you see that tower-light, standing right up out of the sea, like it was set on nothing? Got it? It's far, mind; hard to make it out. That's the Wolf Rock. There's men on that one, too. Waves break right over that one, when it cuts up rough. Think on it."

"You know, I think I'd like to be a lighthouse keeper," says Patrick.

"Terrible life, that is," says Jeremy, bringing out his tobacco tin, and beginning to roll himself a ragged cigarette.

"Wouldn't you be afraid of being lonely?" asks Madge.

"Yes," says Patrick, looking steadily out towards the distant lighthouse tower. "I'm afraid of that more than anything else in the whole world, really."

"Seems a bit perverse to be a lighthouse keeper, then, doesn't it?" says Paul.

"Well . . . but it would have a meaning," says Patrick, quietly. "One would endure it, that thing one feared most, not just because life is bloody, but because one chose to. And it has a reason. One would keep a light that other men find their way by."

83

"Has a reason, that's for sure," says Jeremy. "This is a hard coast for seafarers. Can't think how many ships would come to grief without the lights. And even with them, mind, things happen. Now, when I was a boy, I remember seeing a steamer wrecked on those skerries out there, right beside the light. Wrecked on a clear night, that one was, just a matter of yards from the light. Never did account for that. I've seen some terrible wrecks. One morn when I was a lad there were two of them, sitting side by side on Porthminster sands, right up beside the railway station. Rum sight: torn sails flapping, and the hulls just stranded, sitting there – two on 'em."

"What's the worst you've seen?" asks Paul.

"Ah," says Jeremy. "In thirty-nine the lifeboat went out in weather so bad she capsized just as she rounded the end of the quay. We could see our mates in the water, but we couldn't get to them. She righted herself, and went over again in the next wave. And then again. After the third time there was only one man left aboard her. That was the worst I've seen, young Paul. Now we must be going back along, for I've this and that to see to at home."

"Why are you afraid of being alone?" Madge asks Patrick, in the windy back seat of Jeremy's bus.

"I know what it's like, that's why," says Patrick.

"You've got your family . . . ."

"We're not allowed feelings in my family," says Patrick. "Only thoughts. So if one has any feelings, one has them alone. That's partly why my father can't do with Molly. She has feelings all right – simple ones. But she'll never have anything he would call a thought."

84

Madge instinctively puts a hand to him, meaning to touch his lightly. But he interrupts the gesture by unexpectedly taking her hand and holding it tightly in his. It seems to fit very well. She glances at him, mildly astonished, wondering what he means. Then, "You know, Patrick," she says, "you have very complicated eyes."

"I have *what* eyes?"

"Complicated," she says, beginning to laugh. "They are a sort of green colour, with a darker rim, and then golden amber in the middle. Everybody else makes do with just one colour." But she knows the darkness in Patrick's eyes has nothing to do with the colour. Up in the front seat Paul is talking fishing with Jeremy. Madge begins to sing softly to herself a snatch of song from among the many that drift through her mind:

> "*A ship there is, and she sails the sea,*
> *She's loaded deep, as deep can be . . .*"

"Now don't you go singing as we go by Zennor," says Jeremy, "or the merfolk'll come and take you down among the dead men."

"I don't think you believe half the rot you talk, Jeremy," says Paul. "You can stop playing the crusty old local with us."

Jeremy roars with laughter. The bus comes along the back of Porthmeor beach, threads its way through Downlong, and stops on the harbour-side.

There is a tranquil deep evening on the town, quiet and without a wind. The tide is out, leaving the harbour half full of still, dark water, in which the lights round the harbour-side hang glittering, drawn down into shimmering columns. Bright sapphire shining banners waver below the blue navigation light on the pier; amber stalactites suspended in the cavernous depths of azure water descend below the light on Smeaton's Quay. The sands show just perceptible at the whispering water's edge; a gull still screams overhead. Only if you know exactly where the land lies across the bay can you believe that you can still see the shadow shape of it in the dusk, or make out the white tower of Godrevy where the light shines on and off.

From the quiet dusk on the brow of the hill, over the unlit shrubs and bushes one can see the harbour lying like a scatter of jewels on purple velvet. Gran is outside, standing on the lawn, listening to the distant sound of the waves. She sees a dim glow in the summerhouse, and notices the window open. She goes to shut it. The summerhouse door is ajar. It creaks softly open to admit her. The summerhouse smell reaches her – deck-chair canvas, and grass mowings, and dusty confined air baked dry under the slate roof in the hot sun. In the middle of the floor a candle burns, held in the neck of a wine-bottle, which is submerged under a web of wax like a rock under the edge of a wave. Beside it lies Jim in his sleeping bag, and with him lies Emily, face down, her hair spread out across his pale naked chest. He is sleeping with his arms round her in total stillness. The candle flame burns tall and steady, perfectly vertical.

Gran stops. She looks at them long and shamelessly before turning away, and going out, gently putting the door nearly to behind her. She goes back to standing on the lawn, looking at the view.

Would her father mind? she asks herself. Ought I to do anything about it? And she knows at once, without more than a moment's consideration, that Emily's father would mind. That straightness and simplicity, that perfect candour which he had as a boy has gradually hardened into a habit of thinking and feeling the ordinary things; his frankness has become conventionality. But she knows, also, that he would not expect her to do anything about it; he knows her better than that. He would know she would no more move to change it than to alter the fall of the light, or re-orchestrate birdsong. One should just be pleased, if one can, by events. Gran is pleased. Perhaps, it occurs to her as she goes in, Emily knows me as well as her father does. And not for the first time, Gran feels deeply pleased at herself. She goes slowly, smiling, along the terrace through the open garden door, and asks her son-in-law to put some Tchaikovsky on the gramophone.

"Oh, I meant to tell you," he says, getting up. "We met the burglar on our expedition to Land's End today. And we did invite him to tea. He's a Canadian, over here visiting the scenes of his youth. He'll come tomorrow at four."

"Oh good. How exciting. I'll look forward to that."

"Does it have to be Tchaikovsky?" he asks, getting out a record. "You are a sentimental old thing, aren't you?"

"Yes, dear, aren't I?" she says, still pleased and smiling.

For the last weekend of the reading party a large outing is planned. Not Zennor Hill again; and not Trencrom Hill, for that has been climbed by most of the young men on one afternoon or another during the fortnight. Somewhere further off; Godrevy Point. Everyone would like to see the lighthouse closer to. There is an animated discussion on how to get there, for the two family cars will not hold everyone, and it is some nine miles round the rim of the bay. Mr Jones proposes to hire a car from the garage up the road, and Andrew, it seems, can drive a party in that. Madge and Paul think of the bicycles they used to ride, and go looking in the shed for them. There are four bicycles in the shed, all rusted solid, and with flat tyres.

"We can fix these," says Paul cheerfully. "Ours and one for Patrick. Who shall we offer the other one to? Are any of these weirdies good fun?"

"Matthew is the nicest. He doesn't believe in God," says Madge.

"Christ! Don't you know anything less dramatic about him?" says Paul.

"He comes from Darlington."

"I sometimes wonder about you, Sis," says Paul. "Let's go and offer them, then. We'll need help fixing them all."

Matthew turns out to be very handy at bike-fixing, Patrick to be useless. He can, however, find punctures by holding the inner tubes under water in a bucket, so he is left doing that, while Madge applies glue to the rubber patches, and the other two wield spanners and oil-cans.

"It's going to be heavy going, riding these uphill," says Matthew.

"We could put them in the guard's van on the train to St Erth, and ride from there," says Madge.

The adults are pleased to hear about the bicycles. "It's remarkably kind of you," says Professor Tregeagle to Matthew, "not to mind being separated from the main party."

Matthew pulls a wry face at the professor's departing back. "The main party *is* where we are, so there!" he says, and Patrick laughs.

That night there is a knock on Madge's door. She is propped up on one elbow, reading *Sons and Lovers*, with a secret treat beside her – a huge box of chocolate creams. Thinking it will be Paul, she says, "Come in."

Patrick comes in. He is in a dark red dressing-gown, and holding a half-empty bottle of amber liquid in one hand, and his toothmug in the other. "This stuff is supposed to be good," he says to Madge, conspiratorially. "Why should they have it all? Where's your toothmug?"

"Over there," says Madge, pulling the sheet up over her nightgown to her chin. "What is it, Patrick?"

"Whisky."

"I don't know if I like that," she says. "I've never tried."

"You are about to find out. It says *Glenfiddich Pure Malt* on the label."

"Coo-er. I'm impressed. Or, I daresay I would be if I knew what it meant. Shouldn't we invite Paul?"

"I have. He's fast asleep, flat out. He invited me to go away and leave him be – with considerable emphasis. And everyone else is in bed one whole floor down. None will suspect our midnight orgy!"

"Is whisky enough to make an orgy by itself?" asks Madge, relinquishing the sheet, and relying on her nightgown. "Maybe," says Patrick pouring it out. "Traditionally it goes with cigarettes and wild wild women, to drive one insane."

"Would chocolate creams do instead of cigarettes?" Madge wonders. "Do they go with whisky?"

"One more thing we are about to find out."

"I don't know that I can be a wild wild woman, though," says Madge. "Quiet and thoughtful, and muddled is more like me."

"You seem rather crystal and clear-cut to me," says Patrick, looking at her assessingly. "But in any case, that is Madge-before-booze. Madge-after-booze may turn out wild. Drink up and see."

Madge swigs back a large gulp of the liquid in her glass, and is left gasping with a burning tongue and throat, and tears in her eyes.

"One is supposed to sip it judiciously," says Patrick, looking coolly at her distress.

"*Now* you tell me, you brute – you positively *hairy* brute!" she says, for his dressing-gown displays a triangle of dark hair on his chest, and his wrists, emerging from the cuffs, are decorated likewise with dark brown, growing sideways round their slender shape.

"I'll be beast to your beauty," he says, sipping his mug. "Hey, this is good. Try tasting it slowly."

"It does have a nice taste," Madge says thoughtfully when she has tried again. "It tastes like cornfields look, only very pure and clean," she says. "If only the taste weren't so *ferocious*."

"Him firewater plenty hot."

"Try cooling it with one of these," Madge says, offering her box of chocolate creams.

"I thought you were too good to be true. And I now know that chocolate is your secret vice," says Patrick, taking two.

"It does work, rather well," says Madge in a while, having experimented with alternate mouthfuls of chocolate and whisky.

"You don't think it muddies the pure essence of each?"

"Oh, pooh."

"An adult, I suspect, would be appalled at the thought of eating chocolate with whisky."

"Patrick, what's it going to be like, being an adult? Doesn't it scare you a bit?"

"Well, yes, in a way. But what scares you about it?"

"They seem so different from us; and I don't seem to change much. Can I really be going to be like them? And when will I start to get that way? And shall I find it bearable?"

"What's wrong with just being Madge?" he asks, smiling.

"But I've never known a real adult who was a bit like

me. And how shall we manage to care about the things they care about, and carry their responsibilities?"

"I don't know, I honestly don't," he says gloomily. Then: "I think, you know, they have secret consolation."

"How do you mean?"

"The lucky ones have love for someone. And it makes a private world nobody else can see at all. Then they're all right."

"How do you know?" she asks.

"Well, I don't, in a way. I'm guessing. But take my mother, for example. Her life really is all ground down under caring for Molly. But my father loves her as a carefree pretty person. He gives her clothes and perfumes and bits of jewellery. He makes her a kind of secret self, to be for him, at least – whatever she may have to be for anybody else. I think it will be all right being an adult if we have found someone to love us – and pretty awful otherwise."

"We couldn't just keep the way we are, being ourselves, for ourselves, and not worrying too much?" says Madge, sipping the whisky again.

"Well, I don't *see* why not, but I think not, somehow," says Patrick. "I don't know any grown-up person who seems to manage that. Do you?"

"No," says Madge, after thinking for a while. "We had a history mistress two years ago who fell in love. It made her much nicer to us. She told us a bit about how marvellous he was; and then on prize day he came to the school, and he was awful! Just awful! Positively *fat*! But they kind of shone at each other. So perhaps you're right about a secret world. But then, on the other hand, Patrick, you're making me think about Marie, who was the elder sister of Jenny, my school friend. Marie was at college, and engaged to this student, and he kept buying her books about her subject, and wanting to take her to see cathedrals and Roman ruins, and she would pull wry faces at Jenny behind his back. Jenny was very worried about it. So perhaps it isn't any good having a secret self for someone if it isn't the self one wants to be."

"Well, no," says Patrick. "I should think not. Have some more whisky. And how does one know who one wants to be? I feel all shapeless most of the time. Positively amoeboid."

"So I suppose," says Madge, sipping more whisky, "that real happiness is having one's favourite self, the person one most likes to be, loved by someone. That's quite a thought, Patrick."

"And that's not all, either. Because I don't think it's one's *favourite* self exactly – I mean not necessarily the person one flatters oneself one is, like I fancy myself as a great pianist – I think it's the nearest self – the one one truly is. And I don't think being loved by just anyone will do it either; I think it has to be a special person."

"It seems a lot to ask," says Madge. "Is it all right to finish the bottle?" for Patrick is filling his mug again.

"It isn't finished yet, there's some left. And, well, I think it *is* a lot to ask. I expect it doesn't happen very often. After all, people don't seem all that happy, by and large, do they?"

"I suppose not. Have another chocolate. You know,

93

that's a very different kind of happiness from the sort we've had up to now, isn't it?"

"What *have* you had up to now, do you think? Just put it simply."

Madge grins. "Well it's mostly been being in special places, for me, I think. Places are so detailed and actual; and they last so long. You know they were before and will be after. I'm happy, *looking*, mostly. This is a crummy way to talk, you know, Patrick. Do you think it's the whisky?"

"No," says Patrick. "Not really. I think it's the way we are. I've only known you a couple of weeks, and there isn't anything I wouldn't talk to you about."

"I'd tell you anything, too," says Madge. "And I can't think why!"

"There's all this energy sparking off between us, and it doesn't know where to go yet."

"I suppose *this* couldn't be what it's like to . . . . " says Madge, wide-eyed.

"I don't think so. It isn't what I expect. I feel all tugged about, and tossed up and down. It isn't at all pleasant – it's like changing gear all the time in a car with no synchromesh."

"Well, I'll have to take your word for *that!*" says Madge, laughing. "But it does feel a bit jerky. I think if it went on for long it would be more like being seasick than anything else!"

"Thanks!" says Patrick. He is sitting on the floor at the foot of her bed, resting his chin on the bedclothes, and smiling at her. They begin to laugh, helplessly.

"So I'm like seasickness, am I?" he says after a while, giggling.

"Well, you said I wasn't at all pleasant, blast you!" says Madge, leaning back on her pillow, choking back giggles. "Oh, Patrick, it *is* the whisky! I've got such a funny feeling in my head, like an eightsome reel going on all by itself, and my tummy feels all warm!"

"Well, if it is, then we'll be different in the morning," says Patrick. He gets to his feet, and picks up the bottle and his mug, very slowly, and with elaborate care, as though the floor had become a tightrope under his feet. "Goodnight," he says, smiling. He has a very sudden smile. It creases his lean cheeks, and round his eyes deeply, and he looks years older, and much more carefree while it lasts. He shakes Madge's foot gently where it bulges through the bedclothes, and makes carefully for the door.

"Goodnight, sleep well," says Madge. "Goodnight, sweet prince."

"Typical. That's a bloody quotation," says Patrick, closing her door.

Godrevy morning breaks fine and bright, with a brisk wind blowing, and the wave crests just touched with white across the bay. The bicycle party leaves straight after lunch, shaking free of the bustle of preparations in the kitchen, the piles of rugs and baskets in the porch, and escaping gladly from the fuss.

Beyond Hayle the road rolls up and down, going along

the shore, but out of sight and sound of the sea for the sand dunes lie between. They are grassy and smooth, and shaped as a child might draw a hill, humpy and round, and over them is blue sky with clouds and larksong. The road rolls enough for the rises to be hard work, the dips to be joyous freewheeling. They come to Gwithian, sheltering among its trees, little church, stone cottages, and rooks' nests – so inland a place you could never believe the sea was nearby; and the tall towans keep it from the wind.

On the road beyond Gwithian they are overtaken by the first car from the house – the one driven by Andrew – just before the little bridge descends the slope and crosses the Red River.

"My God, what makes it that colour?" asks Matthew, looking startled at the crimson cloudy waters of the little stream.

"Spoil from the tin mines," says Paul.

"It seems odd it should sound the same as clear water when it looks like that," says Patrick.

"Yes," says Madge, pleased. "It does, rather." But she is eager to go on, to see the lighthouse. And across the stream the road turns suddenly seawards, becoming a rough track that climbs round the hill so steeply that they walk, and push – Matthew unasked pushing Madge's bike as well as his own – until it turns on the height above the beach, and shows them, in a great sweep, the shore: rocks, sands, huge waves, and Godrevy island ringed in white water, just offshore. It stands alone, a short way into the immense vastness of the sea under the sky, that vast theatre on which the light exults, sweeping great streaks of silver across the ocean distances, gleaming on the lovely glassy curves of the rising waves, blinding white on the breaking crests as they avalanche in walls of white foam racing shorewards, transfusing the drift of smoke, as they break, and the spindrift blows off them on the wind. The lighthouse tower is painted white, hexagonal, one of its three visible sides lit brightly, and two in light shadow, softened by reflected brightness from the dancing sea.

Throwing down the bikes, they run along the grassy tops above the rocky beach, and up the path that mounts and mounts the steep promontory, and swings round it till it brings them high up on the outermost corner, overlooking the island, and the light. They can see down into the ring of stone wall around the tower, and onto the grey sloping roofs of its cottages, and outbuildings, and the parched tawny grass where once the garden was.

"When we were children," Madge says wistfully, "there were men on the rock, and they kept a garden. Paul saw it once."

"Only a little thrift, and some wallflowers," says Paul. "Look, Patrick, at that pole sticking up. That's the breeches-buoy they used to get in and out of the relief boat. Still want to be a lighthouse keeper?"

"Glory!" says Matthew. "Whatever for?"

"What do you mean, what for? You know what lighthouses are for!" says Patrick, grinning.

They fall silent, gazing at the sea, the rock, the island below them, and the tall tower rising firm and white to its bright, caged glass eye. The waves play round the rock, filling the foreground with endless movement, with random bursts of white, and the more distant ocean juggles with falling light, keeping a million sequins of sunshine rocking and gleaming and shining back. The four figures seated on the brink of the land hear the cars behind them come near and stop, hear faint voices. Paul gets up and goes to beg a drink for thirsty cyclists who cannot wait till the rugs are spread and the hampers opened.

He comes back with four bottles of fizzy pop and four bent straws. The bottles spew out half their contents on being opened, expressing their disgust at the warm, shaken ride in the car. Patrick, having seen Paul's drink half lost, manages to get his bottle into his mouth a split second after flipping the cap off it, and it fills him with froth, and leaves him gasping for air, and hiccupping helplessly.

A gang of gulls comes wheeling by, screaming overhead.

"Just listen to that vulgar screeching," says Patrick. "And the sky was a nice district before that fishwife crowd moved in!"

"When was that, then?" says Matthew darkly.

"Hark at you!" says Madge. "What could be more vulgar than burping away like you!" Patrick grins, and burps.

"We're not very refined," says Paul solemnly. "Not as elevated as the rest. You really ought to go back there, you know, Matthew, and listen to the philosophy. They're at it already. And that's what you're here for, you lazy dog, not lying about, slumming it with us dummies." He dodges Matthew's mock blow.

"What are they on about, Paul, old son?" says Matthew, lying back comfortably on the grass, with his hands behind his head, and his eyes closed to the sun. "And if it's anything critical, I'll leap up and rush back so as not to miss it."

"Well, don't ask *me*," says Paul. "I'm just a peasant from a County Grammar School; *I* don't understand it. Ask my clever sis. Or the Great Philosophy Professor's son, here. They might know."

"Alas!" says Patrick. "The Great Philosophy Professor, for all his art, cannot transmit his profound insight to his son. Small genetic accident prevents. He doesn't have any luck, genetically."

"Ugh!" says Paul.

"*I'll* have to tell you what they're on about, then, won't I?" says Madge. "Tell me what they were saying, Paul, and I'll expound it."

"Means and ends. Justification of the one by the other," says Paul.

"What sort of ends?" demands Madge. "Bin ends? Bale ends? Loose ends? Journeys' ends?"

"You don't know what ends *means!*" cries Patrick, burping and laughing. "An end, friends, is what we intend. We intend our ends."

"Oh, I don't think so," says Madge. "Surely not. Wished upon us, more likely."

"God, what womanish logic," says Paul. "*I* will explain. When one has an end in view . . ." A gust of wind ruffles them as it leaps inland.

"Hold your skirt down, Madge," says Patrick, "or all

99

this vulgar crowd will have an end in view."

"Speaking personally," says Madge, coolly, leaving her skirt to blow as it likes, "I end in a set of toes. And I like them in view, I like to wiggle them."

"Now if the class will come to attention, please," says Matthew, "I will expound means and ends, and thus prove that, knowing it all already, I have no need to go and listen to all that carefully-chiselled rot, but can stay peacefully idle, lazing about here, putting all thought of it out of my mind."

"Hear, hear!" says Paul.

"Here, here!" says Madge.

"An end," says Matthew, "is an intention. A thing aimed at. Thus you have an end in view – let us say, for example's sake, that you want to visit your aunt in Tooting. To achieve that end you take some means – a train, or a 57 bus, or a long walk. There."

"But what," asks Madge, baffled, "seriously, Matthew, what is interesting about that?"

"Well, Madge, dear child, you know that you are not allowed, repeat, *not allowed* to have a wicked end. That is nasty and immoral and ruled out of court straight away. But what if you have a good end, and the only way of achieving it is to use wicked means? What then?"

"I should think," says Madge, briskly, "it would depend *how* good the end, and how *evil* the means."

"Careful!" cries Matthew. "That is common sense. Common sense will extinguish the discussion, and leave us all confusedly agreed. One must take it to extremes. Suppose, for example, that your end is to save the lives of thousands. Would it be right to do it by killing one man?"

"Such a thing couldn't happen," says Madge.

"I'm afraid it could," says Matthew. "In war, for example. With a hostage. Or with a prisoner who knows where the bomb has been put. Could one torture him?"

"No," says Paul. "Absolutely not."

"So Paul believes in absolute moral values. There are things he would say one must not do, even to save the world. For him the ends do not justify the means. Quite a clear and respectable belief. We could prod him a bit, by thinking of more and more frightful examples of tough situations, so that he will have to sit there consigning his fellow men to endless suffering in order to avoid telling a lie, say, or giving a prisoner a black eye; but if he's a Christian he will stick to his guns; I mean his absolutes. One may not do evil that good may come. That's Paul."

"Well, what's wrong with that?" says Paul.

"Nothing. But it isn't the only opinion. One could go to the other extreme, and find someone who was completely utilitarian. Willing to achieve a good result by any means whatsoever. And while Paul won't torture the prisoner to save a thousand, this other chap will murder ten people if it will make eleven people happy. And then in between there's dear foggy Madge, who thinks it depends; she would do a little wrong, I expect, to do a lot of good, but she would keep a sense of proportion about it. If we asked her enough questions we could find out a lot about her sense of proportion; but once good ends justify just slightly suspect means, you are firmly on the utilitarian, which is to say the practical, which is to say the immoral side of the dispute."

"I can't be expressing myself right," says Madge. "I don't at all think what you describe me as thinking. Happiness can't be what matters most, can it?"

"You mustn't take this personally," says Matthew. "You're just an example, for the sake of discussion. You can have a different set of opinions next time round if you like."

"Good," says Madge.

"What we need is an example. I take it we are all agreed that lying is wrong? Right? Well, then, there you are in your study, peacefully reading *Crime and Punishment*, and a fellow bursts in, crying 'Hide me! Hide me!' and crams himself into your wardrobe. And a few moments later this madman bursts in after him, waving a butcher's cleaver, and yelling 'Where is he? Where is he? Let me get at him, aarghh!' The question is, do you say, 'He's in the wardrobe,' or do you prevaricate, like not answering at all, or standing across the wardrobe door or trying to take the cleaver away, or jumping out of the window, or do you lie like a gentleman, and say, 'He ran out that way just before you came in'? And if the latter, you think the end justifies the means, and in a corner you would probably kill, maim, cheat, fornicate, etc., etc., as long as doing so would achieve some good end or other."

"Don't be ridiculous, Matthew," says Paul.

"I'm not being ridiculous; I'm telling you about means and ends."

"Well, what about a serious example?" says Patrick.

"What about the doctor who came and cured Molly last year, when she was quietly dying in her sleep of some infection or other? What about that?"

"No, Patrick, don't!" says Madge.

"Why not?"

"I think," says Madge, deeply agitated, "you probably shouldn't do philosophy with serious examples!"

"One could only say," pursues Matthew, "that in that case the fellow had got his ends wrong. To-keep-alive-regardless not being a proper end."

"Don't!" pleads Madge. "Please stop!"

"If a person was in terrible agony, and you had the morphine bottle, you'd give an overdose, Madge, wouldn't you?" asks Patrick.

"Molly's not in terrible agony," mutters Paul. "She's bumming about picking flowers."

"*Wouldn't* you, Madge?"

"How do I know what I'd do? I'd do what felt right. But I think . . . what I think is, one shouldn't . . . you see, I don't think one should *calculate*. I don't think one should do sums with good and evil, and what will happen if, and if not. I don't think one ever knows."

"Sort of pacifist position," says Matthew, cheerfully.

"I think one should watch; and be. Not always be tampering, doing things," says Madge.

"Sort of mystical," says Matthew.

"You have a sardonic attitude to the whole damn thing, don't you, Matthew?" says Paul. "What the hell made you study philosophy?"

"Oh, I don't know. It has a sort of fascination about it,

doesn't it, Patrick?"

"Yes it does. One can never decide whether it's the only subject that matters at all, or just a load of abstract crap that doesn't matter a pin. And it has to be one or the other."

"I rather think," says Matthew meditatively, rolling over to prop himself on one arm and look at the shining sea, "that I read it because I like thinking. Like I like playing chess. But Patrick here didn't choose it; it's all round him, like the smell of fish if you live beside the quay. So what do you think, Patrick? Where do you stand among the means and ends?"

Patrick does not answer. He plucks a little stem of grass and looks closely at it.

"Is there *anything* we must not do, regardless of the consequences? Are there absolute moral values?" continues Matthew, exuberantly.

"I think to have absolutes is to blame God for the way things are," says Patrick. "And there is no God."

"We'll have only ourselves to blame if we don't get any grub," says Paul in a little while. "Let's go and get that picnic."

The picnic is not on the cliff's very top, but down the slope, a little way off the brink, to be out of the way of the wind coming over the edge from the sea. The grassy dip in which the party is sitting turns its back on the wide sea, and the lighthouse, therefore, and commands instead a view of the bay; of Hayle towans, the vast expanse of Porthkidney sands, waves and breakers, and the reaches of rusty-pink staining in the sea where the Red River runs out. On the far side of the bay they can see the great bulk of Rosewall hill, and the harbour and town lie indistinguishable beneath it, contre-jour in the afternoon sun.

The picnic party has split into two groups; women and children in one, philosophers in the other, either by accident or by design. The philosophers are holding a colloquium, grouped around their food in various attitudes of formal informality, as though posing to be painted al fresco. Andrew, for example, lies stretched out, head propped on his right hand, at the feet of Professor Tregeagle, who sits rather upright in a folding chair. Beside them Mr Jones sits cross-legged on the rug.

Madge joins the two women, and for a while is happily busy buttering baps, and putting paste and cucumber in them, and handing them round, making sure Patrick gets what he likes, and Paul gets only crab paste, because he doesn't like sardine, and Matthew, whose likes are unknown, gets consulted each time. She makes little squares of cheese to feed Molly, and gives her sips of orange juice. In a while they need to carry plates piled high with buttered baps across to the other group. Madge trots over and back again with more.

"The gist of the Platonic argument is," Mr Jones is saying as she brings the first plate, "that we can look at objects, and judge them to be more or less equal. Yet we can never have encountered two perfectly equal objects, in this world. But knowledge of equality is necessary to permit us to judge things to be more or less equal. Therefore we encountered equality in some previous existence, and have remembered it, though dimly. Our souls therefore existed before our birth, and if they did, may perfectly well survive our death. Plato teaches, remember, the incorporeal nature of the soul."

"It is a strange belief," says Jake, "that a soul must be an incorporeal thinking substance – a ghost in the machine – that consciousness cannot be an attribute of a wholly material being, when, as a matter of fact, every instance of consciousness we know of is, as a matter of fact, associated with a material being."

"Presumably it is the widespread acceptance of Christian doctrine, that makes that commonplace," says Andrew. "For to believe that people are wholly material would be to believe that death was the end, as birth is the beginning."

"Christian doctrine asserts not the immortality of the soul, but the resurrection of the body," says Matthew, arriving with two plates of buns, "which is not at all the same thing."

"So you mean to say that a Christian could believe, as I do, in a completely material view of persons; could think that 'soul' is a word for certain functions of living material beings, and nothing else, and still believe in an after-life, because the resurrected body will resemble the body before death in having the attributes called 'soul'?" Andrew asks.

Fascinated, Madge lingers, listening, and not fetching more food. "Why not?" says Matthew. " We shall sit under the trees in Eden, and talk and eat, and hold hands with those we love, and pass me a ham roll, Jake, please."

"But *who* will, Matthew?" asks Professor Tregeagle. "The difficulty with this view is not that resurrection is impossible, for an omnipotent Deity could re-assemble the elements of a body, and produce a perfect replica of any of us. But, however perfect, that replica would not be the same *me*, the same *you*. God could not make a replica of myself, actually myself, for the same reason he could not make a square circle."

"Bother," says Matthew. "And yes. Why do I always play the religious pieces which always get fool's mate?"

"You're the only one of our number who can play them at all, Matthew," says Mr Jones.

"But it seems obvious to me," Matthew says, "that people are material objects, and I should have thought that the sight of one dead body would be enough to convince anyone of it, unless they were a mad mystic."

But, no, thinks Madge, oh, no, it would not . . . there had been a journey, very early in the morning, bringing her up to the house with a telegram in her pocket, a bird singing in the still garden . . . . "Have you ever seen a dead body, Matthew?" she asks him in a whisper, and he shakes his head.

"It seems doubtful to me if any knowledge of the changes occurring to bodies, including death, can of itself demonstrate that there are no souls," says Mr Jones. "For there are some strong moves from religious pieces, Matthew — there's Bishop Butler's argument. Hold on while I get my notebook."

While he tugs a battered exercise book out of his jacket pocket Madge skips away to bring rolls, and cress, and tomatoes. When she returns, he is reading, "... *for we see by experience that men lose their limbs, their organs of sense, and even the greatest part of their bodies, and yet remain the same living agents*... Then he points out how small we were as children, different bodily, in fact ... and then, *we have several times over lost a great part or perhaps the whole of our body according to certain common established laws of nature, yet we remain the same living agents. When we shall lose as great a part, or the whole, by another common established law of nature – death – why may we not also remain the same? We have passed undestroyed through those many and great revolutions of matter, so peculiarly appropriated to ourselves; why should we imagine death will be so fatal to us?*"

"Oh, but really!" exclaims Jake. The students clamour for a moment, all talking at once, while Madge, her attention fixed, fails to hand round the cress.

Paul and Patrick arrive, commissioned by Mrs Jones to bring the tea flasks and beakers, and pour for the thinkers.

"Well, what did Aristotle think?" asks Andrew. "He must be free from Christian taint. Did he think death would be fatal to us?"

"It's far from simple, I fear," says Professor Tregeagle. "Aristotle defines 'soul' as 'substance-as-concept'. The 'what-it-is-to-be' of something. Matthew's soul is what it is to be Matthew, let us say. Not only living things have this sort of soul – being-an-axe is the soul of an axe. Could we imagine being-an-axe separated from the axe itself? This definition makes nonsense of the idea that soul could exist without body, and therefore of pre-existence, and survival after death. It involves a wholly materialist view of persons, and is quite clear. Unfortunately Aristotle felt obliged to make a most difficult reservation, one might almost call it a retraction, in favour of the intellect, his word 'nous'. Nous is not the same as soul, but is a faculty concerned with truth, which the philosopher takes to be one element in the human, and only in the human, soul. Now I, too, shall read from my notes, like my colleague." He finds a small black leather book, puts on his spectacles, hastily bites a mouthful of sardine-filled bap, and reads, "*Love and hatred are not attributes of the intellect, but of the person who has it, in so far as he does. Hence when this person perishes he neither remembers nor loves, for these things never attached to the intellect, but to the whole which has perished; whereas the intellect is no doubt something more divine, and something more impassive.* Now what shall we say about that?"

"If I understood it correctly, sir," says Jake after a pause, "the intellectual faculty though only possessed by human souls, is possessed *more* or *less* – yet one could hardly be more or less immortal, could one, according to how clever one is?"

"Aristotle does not teach personal, individual immortality; it is not in that context he must be understood," says Professor Tregeagle. "The interesting point is that for Aristotle there remained a division that had to be made between reality which could be attributed to material things, and realities which could not, and that, for him, that division lay not between living and non-living, nor between conscious, and not-conscious, but between the intellectual and everything else."

Round the rim of the grassy hollow in which they are sitting come the two younger Jones children, running. They stumble and laugh, their noise pouring obtrusively into the talk. Behind them comes Molly, chasing, trying hard to catch up, falling back, losing ground. And behind her comes Prudence Jones, walking knees splayed, flat-footed, deliberately aping a clumsy gait. She is dribbling, letting spittle run down her chin, and has her fingers in the corners of her eyes, pulling them upwards and out-wards, dragging her face into a hideous likeness of Molly's. She cannot see where she is going, doing that, and so when Molly gives up suddenly, slithers down the bank, and sits down among the students on the rug, she staggers on, and comes face to face with Patrick, handing his father a mug of tea, and with Professor Tregeagle.

"Put in the balance against that, Wittgenstein's '*The human body is the perfect image of the human soul...*'" the professor is saying.

"Pru! Look out!" shrieks her brother, and she opens her eyes, tosses her head defiantly at her unwanted au-dience, and runs off before her father can catch her. Pat-rick and his father remain frozen, side by side. The tea in the beaker Patrick has given his father slops over a drop or two.

Molly, sitting on the rug, is picking stalks of cress, and putting them carefully between her toes. "Coggletoe.

Petrolpump," she is saying. "Butterknife. Cogito." She looks up at Patrick, and says sweetly and clearly, "Cogito ergo sum."

Everyone stares at her. And Patrick says to his father, speaking in a very soft voice, though Madge, a little distance off, can hear every word, "Well, is that proof good, or isn't it? Because she can say it as well as anyone else!"

"Oh, my God!" says Professor Tregeagle, and with the words come sobs, uncontrollable for a moment, shaking his rib-cage, while he struggles to choke them off, and falls silent, shamed.

"Come, Molly," says Patrick, getting up, and taking her hand. "Come walk. Find flowers."

"Cogito ergo butterknife," she says, trotting off at his side.

Everyone is suddenly very interested in their share of food. They pass plates, and ask each other keenly if they have tried this yet, or that. They need more tea, and Madge, kneeling on the edge of the rug with the flasks, is busy pouring, and cannot, as her soul, if she has one, cries out to do, go after Patrick.

And minutes pass.

Coming up the slope towards the cliff-edge, she meets the wind head-on; it has freshened and is ripping across the grass, tugging at plants and people, and blowing up from the seething water far below, chunks of dirty spindrift, like massive cuckoo-spit. Madge cannot see Patrick. She calls, but the wind whips the words away in the wrong direction. The bright shining sea dazzles her beyond the grassy brink. She begins to run towards the point.

"What's up, then, Sis?" says Paul, catching her up with easy strides.

"I don't know, quite," she says, stopping. "But I feel bad. I think we ought to find Patrick."

"You're rather wrapped up in him, you know, Madge," says Paul. "Are you sure you want to be?"

"Oh, boo, Paul. No I'm not. But I want to find him now."

"I can see, sort of. He's never two moments the same; he thinks the way I swim. You like that. You don't like people to be open and simple, really. Only . . . only he has a sort of downturn to him, Madge."

"Where has he got to, though?" says Madge. They follow the track along towards Godrevy Point, zig-zagging round the bites in the cliff. At first they cannot see the lighthouse at all; it is hiding below the cliff. Then as they go towards it, it appears to rise out of the land, looming up over the grassy shoulder of the hill, eyeing the path; and then as they come nearer still, it recedes again, seems suddenly not near and rising up, but a little way off, standing offshore, with white horses ramping across the gap, and swinging round, breaking into the bay.

No Patrick, no Molly, to be seen.

They turn, and go back the other way.

The land rolls eastwards from Godrevy Point. Little rises lift the path, like a boat going over waves, and finish in headlands; then the path descends and curves inland round a small bay. You can see very little over the edge; but from the headlands you can see the black angry broken chaos of the rocks where the sea has smashed and chewed inland, you can see the waves pawing and crashing to and fro beneath. You can see the precipitous side of the next bluff. The sea draws your eyes always outwards, afar, to an empty horizon; but you need to look carefully where you put your feet on the rough footing of the path. Clumps of thrift and grass lean over and conceal the edge of the fall.

At the top of the second bluff going towards Navax Point, they suddenly see Patrick and Molly ahead of them. Molly is scampering around Patrick's tall lean form, bringing him flowers. He has a big straggly bunch in his left hand.

"Paa-trick!" Madge calls, through cupped hands, but he does not hear. And the wind presses so fiercely off the sea that they all lean outwards, into it, as they walk, to keep their balance against its thrust. Now Patrick is in sight, Madge relaxes. They will catch up with him soon. He is climbing that massive rise ahead. It curves upwards, like a whale's back, rusty brown rocky sides, green-patched like the sea-slimy seals that swim below. On the rock-wall the grass hangs half-way down, a skirt of tattered salt-bleached growth; below that, the sea has undercut the rockface, and the bright light throws cavernous black shadows down to the tumult at the water's edge. A hole in the rock makes a shadow eye on the shark's head out-line of the foreland.

Up the path on the brink scramble Molly and Patrick. She is picking the thrift at the edge, brightly visible in her emerald green dress. Patrick points; she leans out, stooping over the outermost clump of flowers; and behind them both Paul and Madge see Patrick's arm suddenly lifted, see him stretch out towards her as she falls.

Her stumpy little form shoots down the long slide of grass-clad rock, spreadeagles with sudden grace in the free air, and is gone. The overhang of the cliff prevents one from seeing down, and she has made no sound. Madge and Paul break into a run that brings them rapidly up towards Patrick. They cannot see down. Waves and sunlight and wind continue as remorseless as before.

It cannot have happened! says Madge's mind. Desperately it replays the sequence; Patrick points, Molly leans . . . it jerks through again and again.

As they reach Patrick's side the turn in the path has brought them back to face westwards again; over the humped back of the cliff's edge rises Godrevy light – just the top of it, looking over the crest of the land at them with its one dark Cyclops eye.

Running. Screaming. Paul and Madge, crying out to the

adults. The grassy clifftop slides under Madge's feet, rising and falling below her, as though her legs were wooden, as though she floated, and the land raced by.

"There *are* some prohibitions evident even to children and idiots: thou shalt not . . . ." the fragment reaches Madge before her shouts interrupt it. Then everyone is running. There is no trouble finding the particular point on the cliff's edge – Patrick is sitting there, eyes closed, shaking from top to toe, with his teeth rattling audibly together. You cannot see down. There is an overhang.

Matthew reacts first. He is the first to stop staring downwards, and begin a run towards the cars. Madge watches him running away, like a figure in a film (this isn't happening, she is sure!). They hear the car clatter loudly, and fail to start. Once . . . twice . . . then it roars. Matthew drives it straight through the pole gate across the path, and wildly away in a cloud of sandy dust. People standing. One of the undergraduates proposes to climb down. "I forbid you. I forbid that absolutely," says Professor Tregeagle. The wind blows hard off the sea, and whips dry across their faces. The sun slides behind a patch of cloud. Far off, the sea shines silver; nearby, it has a dark gunmetal gleam. It heaves and swoops. A swell is rising. Beneath the next headland they can see the water furious, storming and lashing the land, breaking white, and sucking back again in a long fierce backwash from the teeth of the jagged rocks. But where they are, they cannot see down.

"It is impossible, quite impossible, that anyone could survive that long enough to feel a thing," Professor Tregeagle is saying to his wife. He is holding her in his arms. The sun shines briefly, but another cloud has come up from somewhere, and masks it again at once. Mrs Jones is gathering up her children, taking them away, protesting, loading a car with things. It is Madge who runs after her and stops her taking the rug. She brings the rug, shaken free of crumbs, and puts it round Patrick, across his shoulders and tucked in round his arms, where he is clinging onto himself. He is still shaking.

There is nothing to be done. The group mutters, moves aimlessly, makes twitchy gestures towards each other, falls silent. A lark rises above them, squealing its sharp rejoicing.

Much later they hear a dim thud, like a cannonshot from across the bay. And then another. Relief floods through them. They can see the green stars of the maroons like Roman candles rise above the distant town. They cannot see down. Something will be done: someone has called out the lifeboat.

It looks very small in the water. It comes fast, turning back a deep scoop of surf from each side of its prow. It swings wide of Godrevy, very wide, and then makes a great loop to come in nearer to the tall shore. The group on the cliff can hear its engine throbbing as it sweeps along below them. Paul has taken off his sweater, and tied it by the sleeves to a piece of fencepost. He holds it high in the wind to pinpoint where they stand and lead the rescuers' eyes.

The men are visible in the boat's cockpit, in their bright yellow gear. One of them is scanning the foot of the cliff with binoculars. The boat turns, swings offshore, and beats back again. She keeps her distance off from the cliff. And she comes by again at full speed, while the swell tosses her about. On the third passage along the shore someone points. The boat swings round again, and describes a tighter loop. And then she drops anchor.

At first to the impatient watchers they seem to be doing nothing. The boat rides the swell, up and down. Her engine still drones, although she isn't moving. The wind blows fragments of shout up to the clifftop.

"They're veering down," says Paul, suddenly understanding.

"What? What are they doing?" asks Professor Tregeagle.

"They can't come in too close to a lee shore – with the wind blowing them landwards," says Paul. "They have dropped anchor, and they are paying out the anchor-cable, and easing her towards the rocks. Then when they can reach, they can haul the boat back again against wind and wave by winching the anchor-cable in. It must be very tricky."

"Will they reach?" asks the professor.

"They must be able to see something, or they wouldn't be trying so hard," says Paul. "But it must be bloody tricky."

He is right, everyone can see. The boat tosses and yaws on the swell, more wildly as it is dragged nearer the cliffs.

The clouds have crowded and massed above them. There is a grey evening light, and a steely sheen on the surface of the water below. The lifeboat draws slowly nearer and nearer in.

Patrick is still shaking, and still sits watching.

"Come and sit in one of the cars, Patrick," says Madge. "Don't watch." He shakes his head, and stays where he is.

The boat is on the very edge of breaking water now; almost where the rocks chew up the sea in surf. A surge of backwash takes her hurtling out again; the engine goes into higher revs, fighting against it to keep her steady. She wings up and down on the hump-back of the wave's last rise before it breaks.

Suddenly they see someone in the water. Shouts rise to them, unintelligible. One of the crew has gone overboard on a line, and is swimming, pushing a life-ring ahead of him. Madge's eyes water in the lashing wind as she watches. It seems impossible to swim in that fury beneath; to pick one's way through breaker and undertow, between this black rock and that in the boiling surf. It is unbearable to watch, and impossible to turn away one's gaze. And very soon the swimmer has disappeared under the overhang of the dark rocks below. The muted, wind-scattered shouts continue. Standing in the bows of the lifeboat, a yellow-jacketed figure with binoculars, keeps watch.

"Come away, my dear," says Professor Tregeagle.

"No, no. I must know," says his wife.

And so they all see the life-ring come into view again, with something green tied across it.

"They'd better hurry," mutters Paul. "They'd just

better."

"What's on your mind?" asks Andrew.

"The weather is getting nasty, and there's not much light left," says Paul.

The progress of the swimmer and his burden seems agonisingly slow. Then suddenly a huge wave heaves up, burying the lifeboat completely, and breaking right over everything, crashing up the cliff in a tumult of foam, spraying the faces of the onlookers high above, and retreating in a violent and deadly backwash, leaving waterfalls of foam and hanging mists of spray across the cliff.

The lifeboat reappears, breaking out of the water in a flurry of foam, draining the sea off its sides, floating, netted in a huge web of white cast by the waves, a mesh of spume on the sea. But nothing can be seen of the swimmer or his life-ring.

The stricken onlookers see the crew wind in the broken line. They see, biting their lips, breath held, the anchor-cable paid out another chain or so, the boat strain nearer yet to the mouth of hell. They hear broken cries; see the desperation with which the seas are scanned by the men below. Suddenly Paul spots the life-ring, floating a little way to the right. He shouts in vain; the wind whips his voice landwards. He and Mr Jones run along the clifftop with his home-made flag, gesticulating.

The coxswain sees. The boat is eased sideways; a movement of the swell sends the ring towards it; they lean, they drag it on board. It had appeared to be empty, floating, but a spot of the bright green colour of Molly's dress is visible as it is heaved on board.

The boat stays for another minute or two. Half its crew are anxiously watching the water. But the others are winching in the anchor-cable, hauling the boat out against wind and tide into the deeper water away from the cliff. Painfully, slowly, the boat is inched back. The light is fading; the gleam of the steely sky thrown back off the water is the brightest thing in sight.

At last the boat's engines roar into life again; it swings round, breaking the hold of its anchor, and roars away seawards at last. It goes wide round Godrevy as the light comes softly on, and disappears into the darkening distance.

A clamour of voices, none loud, but many, rises from around Madge as the boat goes off. A crowd of people have gathered unnoticed around them. There are the cars that brought them, in the field below. They surround the reading party.

"Please," says Madge, to Professor Tregeagle, "help me with Patrick," but he hardly seems to hear her. He is leading his wife away, jostling through the crowd of spectators. Jake and Mr Jones help. Patrick seems to be in a state of collapse. He does not answer or speak, and is unsteady on his feet. He has to be helped back towards the cars. A stranger is asked to give him a lift; he is driven away.

"A bad business. Ought not to have been tried, that's what," Madge hears someone saying.

"Who was it in the water, then?" asks another. They are local voices, soft-spoken, concerned.

"It was Stevens, I'm near sure," says someone else.

"Oh, my God, it was Jeremy!" cries Paul, hearing.

"Oh, no!" wails Madge. Let it not be, let it not be, she cries inwardly. Oh, dear God, let it not be anyone Patrick knows!

"Well, 'twould be," the voice is saying. "It would be him, likely. All the others are married men."

People are trooping down from the cliff's edge. The wind has become so boisterous it is hard not to run before it, as it drives them back.

It seems to Madge that she cannot possibly ride her bicycle home. Her knees feel like water, and her ribcage is full of a choking leaden sensation. But there seems to be no alternative. She waits with Paul, while the last few cars drive off. When all is quiet they begin their unsteady ride. Patrick's and Matthew's bikes are left behind.

They start back. The golden light of Godrevy shines out behind them. But it is a flashing light; dark for nine counts in ten. In the twilight they see the curious colour-change on the waters of the bay, the rusty-pink cloudy staining where the Red River runs out, where the land bleeds silently into the sea. Half way to Hayle a car coming up the road stops by them; Matthew has come back to bring them home. They load the bikes on the roof-rack, and Matthew struggles with a strap to keep them secure.

"Oh, Paul, what will happen to him?" murmurs Madge, as they gratefully get into the car.

"They'll go and look for him when the wind drops. Most likely he'll be washed up somewhere in a day or two," says Paul, huskily. He takes her hand, and holds it.

But it was about Patrick that Madge had meant to ask.

There is a policeman in the drawing-room. He has a notebook. He is speaking kindly. "I am very sorry to intrude on you at a time like this, but if you could just tell me what happened exactly . . . ."

"I wasn't there, I saw nothing; my son was with the child," says Professor Tregeagle. "And you cannot speak to him now, I'm afraid. He is in a state of shock. What he says is not making any sense at all, and the doctor has given him sedation. Tomorrow, if you really must."

"Perhaps I need not insist," says the officer, "for among so many of you, surely somebody saw what happened?" But everyone is looking blank.

"I saw," says Paul. "And so did my sister." At once all eyes are on them. Madge feels the ground sway beneath her. How terrible of Paul to offer . . . she should have spoken to him on the way home, even with Matthew listening, should have begged him not to tell . . . but she knows it would have been useless to ask Paul to deny the truth.

"Patrick was walking with Molly along the cliff-edge path," says Paul. "We could see them ahead of us. Molly went very near the edge after some flowers growing there, and Patrick tried to grab her, but he just didn't catch her in time, and she fell off the edge." Madge's head swims. She can hardly believe . . . Paul *is* lying! He is lying, un-asked, out of sheer good will.

"Patrick Tregeagle tried to catch hold of Molly, and just missed her . . . are you certain of that, young Fielding?" asks the policeman.

"Oh, *quite* certain. I saw his arm go up and stretch towards her. Madge will tell you; she must have seen it too." And it is borne in on Madge that Paul is not lying; Paul is telling the truth according to Paul. He tells what he saw; it is what she saw that is untellable.

"I saw the same as my brother," she says. "It happened just as he says."

"Well, then, we shan't need to disturb the young man," says the policeman, putting away his book. "Two witnesses will do for tonight. There'll be an inquest, sir, a double one I shouldn't wonder, when they find poor Mr Stevens' body. Your son will have to give evidence at that, sir, and so will you, and the two young Fieldings. Would you bear that in mind, sir, when making plans for the next week or so?"

Madge escapes, and clambers up the stairs. She sits down in the window-seat of her attic, facing the sea. She is miserable and confused, and dazed. Paul did not lie, she tells herself; he saw – since he says so – Patrick try to save Molly and fail. But I saw Patrick push her over; there's no denying that's what I saw. And I can ask myself over and over if I'm not just nasty-minded, if Paul isn't probably right, and I know he isn't. He has such a loving nature, such an open unclouded sort of mind, he would never see evil unless he had to. I am the one who saw. . . .

The wind is roaring now, rattling the window. Madge leans forward to open it and slam it tight shut, and in with a gust of cool air comes the sound of the sea, the voice of angry surf, and angry wind. She shivers. A moon is rising, masked in bright-margined cloud. Godrevy light shines out. Keep away, it says. Don't come here. And somewhere in the dark waters around it there is a brave man drowned . . . .

I saw Patrick commit murder! Madge cries to herself. And I lied about it. I said without any hesitation that I had seen what Paul saw, and I will lie again, and again, and swear false oaths about it. I am the one who lies to protect the fugitive from the madman, and who, Matthew said, in a corner would lie, kill, maim, cheat, fornicate, to gain some good end or other. Patrick is a murderer, and I am his next of kin.

Outside the wind frets and howls.

To entertain the burglar Gran has spent the morning making seed-cake, and scones, and fresh lemon curd. She is still amused at having invited him, and he is another cup to pour; the more there are, the more she feels queen of the tea-pot.

The burglar is indeed, as she had been promised, distinguished and handsome. He is tall, with grey hair and a slight trace of transatlantic accent.

"This is my ancient mother-in-law," says Tom, bringing him in to the living-room. "Dr Henderson, Mother."

"How nice," says Gran. "Do sit down. This is my daughter, Harriet, and this is Emily, my niece, and Jim, her young man."

"Your niece?" says Dr Henderson, surprised at Emily.

"Yes indeed," says Gran. People are often surprised, and she likes to tell them. "My brother is a little younger than me to start with, and then he married for a second time rather late in life. Emily is the only child of that second marriage. And that . . . sugar? . . . milk? . . is how she comes to be so deliciously young for her aunt. Or, contrariwise, how she comes to have an aunt so inordinately *old*. Do have some curd on your scone, Dr Henderson, I made it myself, and it really is very nice indeed."

"Thank you, I will," says Dr Henderson, settling comfortably into a chair, and arranging his plate and cup on the little table beside it.

"And now you must tell us why you have been lurking round our gate," says Gran.

"Lurking? Oh, hardly that! Just passing by and looking in."

"*Lurking.* We have even christened you the burglar, so full of intent was your loiter."

"Damn me!" he says. "What do you know!"

"What we want to know is, what do you mean by it?" says Gran sternly.

"I'm on a visit from Toronto," he tells them. "I was returning to the scenes of my youth, in a way. You see, I once spent a summer vacation here and I've been trying to decide if it was in this house. But I promise I'm not a felon of any kind."

"Of course not; you hardly look the part!" says Tom.

"Now I wonder when that could have been?" says

Gran. "Odd, that. It must have been very long ago, Dr Henderson."

"Oh it was. I, too, am inordinately old." He smiles at Emily. "And I don't remember a thing about the inside of the house I stayed in. All gone."

"Come outside, and see if that helps," says Gran. She leads the way into the garden.

Standing on the terrace, looking at the wide lovely view, he says quietly, "You know, I had forgotten the sea."

"Forgotten the sea?" says Gran. "Then it can't have been this house."

"I don't mean I have forgotten whether you could see the sea from where I stayed; I mean I had forgotten what the sea is like to look at. All these years I've kept away from it. I had remembered that it is frightening, and forgotten how beautiful . . . . There. I must remember that I am now in England, where people don't talk like that."

"Don't talk like what?" says Emily, arriving.

"Don't much say what they feel, I think," he says.

"Oh, it always depended *who*, however far back you remember," says Gran.

"I'll bet!" says Emily. "Can't imagine *you* tight-lipped, Aunt, at my age."

"Cheeky monkey! Go and get me some more tea, Em, will you? And for our guest, too."

"There was a dramatic lifeboat incident the year I was here," says Dr Henderson.

"That hardly serves to distinguish one year from another in this place."

"A dreadful thought."

"It *is* beautiful," says Gran, looking at the horizon. "Never more so than when it is terrible. It takes a fool not to be afraid of it."

"Yes."

"But you have kept away from it for years. I wonder why?"

"I hardly know. I'm not afraid of heights, or of spiders."

"Well, well," says Gran. "I think one cannot know what one is afraid of until a crisis arises. When it does, like as not, one manages to do what is required."

"You mean that kindly," he says, shaking his head. "But I *do* know the sea is too much for me." She says nothing. In a while he says, "I was staying once in a seaport, in terrible weather. It was a small town, with only two hotels, and the hotel porter was the lifeboat secretary. I had signed the register as Dr Henderson – it's an academic doctorate, you know, nothing to do with medicine. By and by the lifeboat coxswain came to me and asked me to go out in the boat with them. They had to get a fisherman with an injured spine off a deep-sea trawler, and they needed a doctor. The local man was delivering a difficult baby. I said no, I wasn't a doctor . . . ."

"But for Christ's sake," says Tom, arriving carrying the extra tea, and followed by Emily, "if you weren't, you weren't."

Dr Henderson looks ruefully at Gran. "I had been trained in mountain rescue," he says. "I would have known how to get a man onto a stretcher and give scratch first aid. I could have told them that, and gone with them."

"But if you were only a visitor, passing through . . . it had nothing to do with you."

"That's what I thought at the time. Not my problem. But I've thought about it now and then, since. And when you think about it, why should the hotel porter go? Or the greengrocer's second son? Or the fisherman who has had the sense to get his own boat in out of the storm? Or the local doctor, who, if he could have finished his breech delivery in time, would have cleaned up hastily, got into oilskins, and gone into the teeth of the easterly without a moment's thought?"

"They go because drowning in raging water is so horrible a fate," says Gran. "And going, they risk it for themselves. It has a terrible symmetry."

"I should have gone," says Dr Henderson.

"Yes," says Gran.

"What happened to the fisherman, Dr Henderson?" asks Emily suddenly.

"Oh, he was all right. They managed very well without me, as it happened. But that doesn't make any difference to me."

"Made plenty of difference to him," mutters Emily tartly.

"Are you spending long in this country?" asks Tom, brightly. "And what's Canada like?" He steers the conversation on to safe English subjects for another half-an-hour.

When Dr Henderson takes his leave, Tom sees him to the door. "What do you do in Toronto?" Tom asks, as he hands the departing guest his coat.

"I teach philosophy," says the burglar.

The storm wind sobs and moans over the night roofs of Goldengrove. It tears itself to shreds on the gutter corners and sharp gable ends, and howls with pain. Lying in the attic bed one is submerged in a tide of sound, a cockle on the ocean floor, listening to the fury above. Closed safe and tight in a shell of sheet and quilt, Madge listens. The banshee wailing of the wind cannot drown the other sound; the sound of Patrick sobbing. Madge listens for a long while before getting up and going into Patrick's room. She sits in the battered cane armchair under the window, and folds her hands in her lap, and listens. A little moonlight makes ghost outlines in the room. Of Patrick she can see only the shadowy darkness of his tousled head on the pillow.

"I loved her," he says, chokingly, after a while.

"Yes," says Madge softly. "Of course you did."

"Oh God, how horrible. Oh, God, I'm mad, mad. I killed her!"

"You're not mad, Patrick."

"I wanted . . . Oh, how could I?"

"Are you *sure* you did anything? You know, Paul and I saw her fall, and Paul is usually the calm observant one. I thought you had pushed her, but he thought you had grabbed to stop her falling, and just missed. Couldn't you perhaps have done that?"

"I don't know," says Patrick, miserably. "The awful fact is I just don't know. The moment I had done it, I didn't feel quite certain, couldn't remember – Oh, God, Madge, do you think one could murder someone and forget it instantly?"

"Hush, Patrick, try to keep calm. If I get you some hot milk, would it help you sleep?"

"I'll never see her again," he says. "I murdered her!"

In the morning comes the first of five bleak, dreadful days. The reading party disperses as rapidly as possible, catching the lunchtime train, with cases and boxes of books. Unasked, and making no comment, Matthew stays, and waits quietly in the background. And those who will be needed for the inquest must stay until the sea spews up the missing body. Six of them in the suddenly quiet house, and each with a raw spot that the others fear to touch.

Mrs Tregeagle bears the waiting best. She keeps to her room for three days, is seen red-eyed. But then she is tranquil, and more than tranquil. Madge thinks she is slowly unfurling, like a florist's rose freed from cellophane. She is more herself – well, more like somebody. She goes for walks. She asks Madge what the heights are called, and where the funny street names in Downlong come from. People are kind to her when she goes out; she finds she can say to them, "Molly cannot have felt any-thing. If it weren't for that poor man . . . ." A great burden has rolled from her, and the future no longer hangs over her like death. It isn't, Madge perceives, that she didn't love Molly; it isn't that she isn't grieving, for she is. But grieving for Molly is a good deal easier than living with the thought of her there for ever, growing larger, stronger, more unruly . . . and it's a good thing, really, that Mrs Tregeagle feels like this, Madge thinks, for it is the only small good effect to flow from Patrick's great attempt at action, at manipulating the universe, at refusing to leave things be and blame God.

Madge listens while Mrs Tregeagle talks of a large gift to the Lifeboat Funds. Unasked and unnoticed, she re-moves Molly's things, a few clothes, a few battered toys, and gives them to the Methodist Jumble.

"I *expected* to feel dreadful. I expected to feel crushed by guilt," Patrick tells Madge, in the dead of night. She is sitting in the chair beside his bed, where he lies face down, his voice half muffled in his crumpled pillow. "I knew I would. And I thought that was nothing, nothing com-pared to what she would suffer as she grew to know dimly what other people felt about her. She wasn't as bad as they thought, Madge, she was going to partly know . . . she had a mother who just despaired about her, and a father who thinks the intellect is immortal, and souls resemble bodies . . . and me. I couldn't see how one protected her

131

for ever. I hated that doctor more than anyone in the world, that man who kept his own conscience clean by keeping her alive at *whatever* cost to her and everyone else. I thought I ought to be willing to suffer guilt for her sake. Doesn't that sound right? Is that so wrong?"

"I don't know, Patrick," says Madge. "I can't tell. It isn't how I think."

"I'm still not sorry about her!" he says defiantly. "I'm not! But I hadn't expected to harm anyone else . . . Jeremy . . . . Oh, I didn't mean to . . . ." He is weeping again.

But unexpected things happen every day, thinks Madge. How can one not expect them? How can one leave them out of account?

"You didn't mean to hurt Jeremy, Patrick," she says. "And people usually feel guilty only about what they meant, don't they? Try to sleep."

"I shall pay," he says. "I shall tell the inquest I pushed her, and they will lock me away, safely, where I can't do any more harm."

"Oh, God, Patrick, no, you mustn't!" says Madge. "Go to sleep. Think it over in the light of day."

Paul grieves very quietly. Only Madge knows he is doing it at all; but then, Madge always knows what Paul feels.

"It makes you see how shaky things are," he says to her as they roam together along the golden shore. "When a person who has always been there suddenly isn't. The world seemed safe and solid and as though it had always been what it is; now I feel it's paper castles."

And Jeremy had always been there, Madge reflects, as certain as the scenery. Not quite fixed, but recurrent, like the blue and green swathes of nets that drape the quay, organic, an emanation of the local ecosystem. And, Madge sees, he was Paul's root here, Paul's more than hers, but hers also; he was the one whose friendship picked them out of the hordes of visitors and made them belong, gave them not-strangers' faces. Once, a year or so back, there was an upcountry tripper on one of Jeremy's fishing tours round the bay. He was throwing his weight about, showing off his local knowledge. "Have you been to Hell's Mouth? Have you climbed Trencrom Hill? You ought to you know ..."

And in a while Jeremy cut in past Paul's patient, "Yes, actually, more than once ..." and said, "Young Fielding's been coming here since way back. Good as local, he is." And the man was silenced. Now Jeremy is gone, we are just trippers, Madge thinks, sharing Paul's pain; like any visitor who comes and goes, and prefers Mevagissey, or Helford.

"He was the only real person I have ever known," says Paul. "The only one who earned a living in a proper way in the world. I wish he had kept his boat. If he still had his boat I would buy it, somehow."

"What would we do with it?" murmurs Madge.

"I am damned ..." says Patrick, with his teeth chattering

in his head. "Oh, God, I thought that if there was no hell, one couldn't be damned . . . I was wrong . . . I am in hell . . . ."

And he really is, Madge sees. *Where is the head that hath no chimeras in it?* That a harpy is not a centaur can be as certain knowledge as the propositions of Euclid. And Patrick can be damned.

"Hell is just true in a different way," he says, lying still enough, but staring horribly at the ceiling. "In a nearer and more dangerous way, and I am . . ."

Madge, shivering a little in her thin nightgown, searches desperately for a thought with which to wrestle for Patrick's soul. "I don't think a person could be damned," she says, "while there is still something more awful than anything they have done, which they still shrink from doing. That's what I think."

"I keep seeing faces staring in the shadows on the ceiling," says Patrick. "They keep me awake . . ."

"Come on, then," she says. "Try my bed, the ceiling's different." She leads him to the other attic, and tucks him into the warm hollow in her bed which she left when she went to see him minutes ago.

"There," she says. "Better?"

"What is left?" he asks. "What could be worse?"

"Telling your mother what you did would be worse," says Madge. "That would be really damnable." She sees the stare go out of his eyes as he begins to think about that. "So you can't tell that inquest *anything*, Patrick," she says. "You tell them just what Paul said. You have to. Now I'll get you a drink, if it would help you sleep."

Later she climbs into his vacant bed. The sheets are all tangled up, and a faint skin-smell lingers on the pillow.

"Miss Fielding," says Professor Tregeagle. "Can you spare me a moment alone with you? Thank you. We are, that is, my wife and I are very grateful to you for being so kind to Patrick. You seem to be the only one who can calm him."

"There's no need to thank me," says Madge, blushing, and wanting at once to escape.

"I understand how Patrick feels – at least I think I do. He was the one in charge of Molly when it happened. But of course it could have been anyone. It is impossible to be alert a hundred per cent of the time; it was always on the cards that something terrible would happen to her. It is Patrick's misfortune that he was the one . . . . That is what's upsetting him, Miss Fielding, isn't it?"

"Why don't you ask him?" says Madge.

"Of course. I, er, just meant . . . Madge, is there anything you know about what happened, that I ought to know?"

"There is nothing I ought to tell you," says Madge carefully, after a moment.

"My dear girl, why, after all, should you trust me? But believe me, I love my son dearly, and I am very concerned about him. Half the time he seems out of his mind over all this. He called himself a murderer in my hearing . . . I take it he is raving when he says that."

I am almost sorry for him, floundering around like this, thinks Madge. Almost, but not quite. Still, he is Patrick's father.

"I think he felt like killing Molly," she says at last. "And then the accident happened, and because he had felt like doing it, he thinks perhaps he did do it." And how plausible that sounds, she thinks as she says it. I must try it on Patrick.

"Why did he feel like killing her?" asks Professor Tregeagle. "We loved her in spite of . . ."

"Oh, you *wouldn't* know!" cries Madge. "You wouldn't know anything. Actually sitting there, going on about children and idiots, about how pure intellect is the immortal part, and a person's soul resembles their body – actually saying that in *front* of everyone, actually while Molly's ugliness is being guyed. Don't you think people have feelings, or do you just think they don't matter?"

"Oh my God," says Professor Tregeagle. He sits down abruptly, and his tranquil clever face suddenly wears an expression like Patrick's. "But that's absurd . . . . Madge, that isn't what we said. What we said doesn't *mean* that . . ."

"Whoever are you to say what it means?" she asks him. "It means what it does mean, and you can't stop it. You can sit around all you like, like a stage army muttering Wittgenstein instead of rhubarb, and saying to words, 'Thus far shalt thou mean, and no further, and here shalt thou break thy swelling waves.' It doesn't make any difference. The words mean what they mean to Patrick as much as they mean what they mean to you."

"Patrick never could be clear and cool. Never could grasp an accurate definition. It's just like him to make a vast emotional mess of an intellectual discussion. If we ever gave him a gun he'd point it backwards."

"Do you know something?" Madge says, regarding him coldly. "Do you know why you are here? Because my headmistress thought clever company might do me good, might help to make me decide to try for an Oxford scholarship. But that was a big mistake. I've just decided to be a hairdresser, or work in Woolworth's."

"My dear, whatever you think of us," he says, suddenly recovering a little calm, "don't spite yourself because of it. You are quite clearly a clever girl. You mustn't waste that."

"Oh, Christ," says Madge. "Can't you think of anything else at all?"

Patrick on the fourth day, quite calm, walking round the house and garden with a waxwork face. "I have accepted it now," he tells Madge. And when he says it they are standing below the garden gate, on the last turn of the path up to the house, looking down at the beach and beyond. Against the deep blue ocean, Madge sees as he says it the grey and white, tawny-white, gullfeather-coloured town, nestling like a folded wing on the curved back of the hills, on the green slopes of the Island, and in a downy drift around the bright shore, so that for ever afterwards whenever she remembers what he said, until she is an old woman, she remembers also the soft light of one warm hazy summer day.

"You can stop worrying, Madge," he says. "I have accepted what I did. I won't own up at the inquest."

"Good," she says. "It wouldn't do any good."

"I am a murderer," he says, quite camly. "I shall be in hell till I die. And alone. For my true self, my nearest self, is the one that killed Jeremy. So unless I deceive them about who I am, no one will ever love me."

"Oh, no, Patrick," says Madge. "No, no. They will. I will."

Paul on the fourth day insisting on taking Madge off with him, insisting on getting her alone, walking her off to Carbis Bay on the lizard-baking rocky path between the railway and the sea.

"I like him, too," Paul tells her. "I can see. He is interesting. And then you've always been a goose about our suffering brethren, haven't you, Sis? Do you remember that perfectly frightful blind man you got taken up with one summer? You're a sucker for wounds, Madge, like a tin of Elastoplast."

"I thought you were going to say like a vampire, after that!" she says, trying to make him laugh.

"Huh, huh," he says. "No, you must listen. Because I have to say this to you. You can't do anything about Patrick. When he's got over this, it will be some other damn thing. He's just the sort of person who leads an unhappy life. You do know that, don't you?"

"Like his namesake, you mean, driven and hounded and condemned forever to weave ropes of sand on the shore?"

"Do I sound melodramatic? Well, I can't help that. I don't do it often. But you do know, Madge, don't you? You know you can't make him happy, and very likely he'll make you as miserable as he is."

"Yes, Paul love, I know," says Madge. The rocks run out under the sunshot shallows of the sea's edge below them, blotching green and turquoise with patches of purple. On the grass where they sit, the thrift grows, and the yellow vetch. And far out, in the distance, the light-house in a tissue of haze is just visible.

Madge sighs. She does know. She sees ahead of her a life on the brink of the abyss. It will be all in Patrick's troubled mind, the terrible precipices on whose knife-edge of nightmare fall she will have to tread – *Hold them cheap may who ne'er hung there* – and for a moment she wavers, and thinks longingly of the shadowless tranquility of being with Paul.

"Look! There's a cormorant," he says. Patrick wouldn't have seen it; he doesn't much notice where he is, she muses.

"I do know, Paul," she says.

"But it doesn't stop you?"

"No." For when someone needs love and comfort, one has to go. Hasn't one? Would Paul really turn his back? Could there be much to choose between counting the cost, as he recommends, and that insane calculation of good and evil that brought Patrick where he is? She remembers Jeremy once showing her a picture in a lifeboat manual of the gold medal, the highest award for gallantry of the R.N.L.I. It showed a naked man being drawn out of the water into a boat. *Let not the deep swallow me up*, it said.

"I could explain to Jeremy better than I can to you," she says, her eyes suddenly full of tears.

Matthew on the fourth day, trying to calm an agitated Paul. "Don't worry. Come for a swim. No, of course you can't reason with her, she doesn't work like that. She works on instinct. And there's nothing wrong with that."

"I thought thinking was a good thing. At least according to you," says Paul.

"It's all right for some. Madge doesn't need it. Her feelings lead her right."

"Christ, another nutter!" says Paul. "Damn being led right. I'm afraid she'll be led unhappy."

"Oh, I don't know," says Matthew. "She might well cheer Patrick up. Wouldn't anyone be cheered up? I wish she felt sorry for me!"

"Feeling-sorry-for isn't the same as loving, you poor fool," says Paul.

"Oh, one thing leads to another, often enough," says Matthew. "I'm leaving on the evening train. Tell your sister, in case I don't see her again, that I'll call on her in London some time and take her out to tea."

Patrick on the evening of the fourth day, pacing his room, still unable to sleep.

"God, it's hot in here!" says Madge, arriving in her dressing-gown. "Let's go out."

"My mother will fuss like anything if she hears me go down," he says. "She's *concerned* about me."

"Out here," says Madge, opening the little door.

In the roof valley they stand side by side, under a thick sky pierced with stars. The sound of the sea comes clearly to them from far below, in the hushed night.

"You can't, you know," Patrick says after a while. "You just can't mean what you said."

"I can."

"Any minute you'll see through me, and go away in disgust."

"You don't have to worry about that," she says. "I see through you now, I think."

"And you don't mind?"

"Don't mind what, Patrick, dear? Who are we to mind each other?"

"My horrible bleeding self-pitying soul."

"The human body is the perfect image of the human soul," she says, and puts her arms round him.

On the fifth day Jeremy's body is found washed up under Gurnard's Head, and the ordeal is about to be over.

Emily comes, running lightly down the garden, jumping the lavender hedge instead of going down the steps, her long hair swinging down her shirt, to find Gran dozing in a deck-chair specially set in a sheltered spot and facing the lovely view through the garden gate left open. She likes that prospect; it reminds her of a painting called *The Blue Door*, or was it a window? but anyway.... She wakes when Emily's shadow casts coolness on her face.

"Please, Aunt," says Em, "the rain came in through the belvedere roof in *floods* during that storm, and all Jim's things are wet. I don't think he ought to sleep out there another night, or he'll catch his *death*. And I don't like to tell Harriet because she made such a bother about it when we got here . . . so I was wondering if I could clear a space in the attic, just a small space. Would you mind?"

"No, dear, of course I wouldn't," says Gran. "Can't have him catching cold. And I think I'll come too, you know, and help you. What fun! We never know *what* we might find!"

"Ah, no, Aunt, it's a pity to spoil your rest. You must snooze off again, and let me do it. And I promise to bring you the three most fun things we find there. Will that do?"

"Yes, Em dear, that would be lovely," says Gran, settling back into her chair. It seems only yesterday she would have leapt up and climbed up the stairs two at a time, and gone rummaging joyfully through dusty boxes. And one's mind takes it hard, she thinks; one's soul is as lithe as ever, and as volatile, and is amused, patronising and irritated by the body's decrepitude.

An aged man is but a paltry thing . . .

yet inside I feel no different; I feel the same as ever, or rather, which is more important, as many different things as ever . . .

A tattered coat upon a stick, unless
Soul clap its hands and sing, and louder sing
For every tatter in its mortal dress . . .

though it isn't monuments of magnificence for me (yet Santa Sophia is more like a vision than a building, I do remember), it's more the brightness falls from the air, the eternally changing sea, and the view of Godrevy light. Yet what could this be inside me, that feels unchanged, through so many and so great revolutions of matter? And, do you know, in all the talk I ever heard about the immortal soul, I never recall the eternal youth of the inner self brought in evidence against us being all bodies . . . odd that. Well, not so odd, really, for it's the old in their ramshackle frames who know it so clearly, and it's young men who bother about the immortal soul . . . I ought to know better at my age. Ghosts in machines, indeed – whoever believed in ghosts? And I think after all I'll take myself upstairs and help Emily. I shall go very slowly. I'll get there.

Little by little. Up the stone steps Emily by-passed, one

by one. Past the straggling overgrown bush of Rosa Mun-
di, past its best long ago, should have been cut down, but
Gran likes it. And slowly along the narrow terrace, between the catmint and pinks and lavender, towards the
corner of the house where the view is best, because it is
easier to go right round than to climb the steep flight of
steps to the French windows of the dining-room. And as
she goes, here behind her come pattering sandalled foot-
falls. Young Peter, and Sarah, and small Beth racing after
her, calling "Gran! Gran!" and eyes shining.

And Madge turns round, and stoops, and picks up her
grandchild, and holds small Beth up to look at the view,
just for a moment, for even this slender, bird-boned child
is heavy for her to hold now.

"I like how this place cuddles the sea," says small Beth.

"Why, yes, Beth, so it does," says Madge smiling. "I
like it too."

"Gran, Gran," says Sarah. "Listen to the bell counting
one. Why is it?"

"It's tolling, dear. For somebody's funeral."

"Who's dead?" asks Peter.

"One is not supposed to ask for whom it tolls," says
Madge.

"Sorry, Gran," says Peter solemnly. "I didn't know
that."

And, oh Lord, thinks Madge, now what have I said?
Misleading the poor child . . . .

"About death," Peter continues. "I think it's all a bit
crummy, you know, Gran . . . ."

But here comes Emily, arriving, laughing, wearing a

Paisley shawl rotted into ladders all over, and a huge pink garden-fête straw hat with a moth-eaten white rose, that Madge wore decades back, one summer, and holding in her hand a little brown bottle. Behind her comes Jim, her attentive shadow.

"Wow! Hey, how do I look, everyone?" cries Emily, dancing round them.

"Like a prehistoric lady," says Sarah.

"Can I have the bottle, Aunt?" asks Emily.

"Goodness!" says Madge, taking it. "That's been lost for ages. I'm very glad to see it again; it always did make me feel special. And no, Em love, I think I'll keep it. You can have it when I'm gone, if you like."

"Heavens, Aunt, it's only an old brown bottle with no cork!" says Emily.

"Don't worry, Em, you won't have long to wait," says Beth. "She's awfully old."

"You shouldn't *say* that, Beth," says Peter.

"Tell me about the bottle, dear funny Aunt," says Emily, taking Madge's hand. And for all I'm so different from Paul, and always was, thinks Madge, his daughter is quite like me.

"The sea gave it to me, dear," she says. "And in all the years I walked on its edge, and watched it, it's the only sign it ever gave of liking me."

"It washed it up at your feet, you mean?" asks Jim.

"Three times. Twice I threw it back. The third time I kept it. It's a very *nice* bottle, you know."

"Yes, Aunt, it is," says Emily, smiling. "I would very much like it when you're dead. Thank you. I'll put it in your room for now." And off she goes, whirling Jim after her, round the house, out of sight.

"You see, Gran, what I want to know about death, is," pursues Peter remorselessly, "is what's the point? I mean it does make it rather pointless, doesn't it, people just getting born and then dying all over the place? I mean, I don't believe all that stuff about resurrection, because people rot, don't they, when you bury them? And it seems if they just keep on dying, millions of them, well, what's the point of being alive in the first place?"

What can I say? thinks Madge. Of course, he's right. We die, and when we die we rot, and that's an end of it. I have never had any doubts of that. And yet . . . it's an odd thing, but it's not the romantic opinion about the departing soul that is shaken in the actual presence of death . . . in the actual presence of death it is the rational belief in mortality that is shattered. I do remember that quite clearly. Twice I have seen it. It was my dear Patrick once, but before that, long before, it was my own grandmother . . . .

There had been a journey. A night journey, in a train with prickly plush head-rests that indented my leaning cheek. It was very early in the morning, only just after dawn. The train chugged under Carrack Gladden, and not a single footprint on the wide, wide open sands, only the white waves moving. From the station to the beach, my footprints on it first, winding along the waves' edge. When I reached the house, when I turned my key in the door of the shuttered silent house, I had taken off my shoes. My naked feet left ghost prints on the polished floor. I stretched out my hand to the polished doorknob, and went into the living-room. It was darkened, the curtains drawn. A table had been brought into the middle of the room, with a white cloth on it, and my grandmother was laid out on the table under a white sheet. Her face was uncovered. There was an unutterable silence in the room. One would believe it was slowing one's own heartbeat, stilling one's own pulse. I cannot recall anything I thought or felt, except that appalling stillness.

I had come too late. Had I expected to be in time? I don't know. Travelling to a death would always be undiscovered country, from which no traveller returns unchanged. I have never forgotten how it dislocated my certainty. It was my grandmother on the table. Can one have any idea how intensely local, how particular to one person a body is, till one has seen a not-living one? And yet, how totally, how overwhelmingly, how absolutely, I knew *she is not here*. This "her" is empty of her utterly. It has nothing whatever to do with her, is husk, shell, having her shape in every detail. Here, where she always was, she is not now. The stillness so complete it quenches out of me everything, every flicker of feeling or thought, except awe. And – how can one help it? – since she is not here, one wonders where, then, is she? Where has she gone? *Where is she now?*

I sat in a straight-backed chair beside her for a long time. Until the morning sun ruled golden lines across the room from between closed shutters, and Amy, my grandmother's maid, found me there, and tutted and fussed over me, and made breakfast, and wept a little. I was dry-eyed, and with an immortal calm upon me. And I have never forgotten it. That the survival of the soul is a commonplace deduction from the sight of a dead body. In the presence of death it is mortality that seems preposterous. I am still puzzled by that, still awestruck. Who could believe in souls? I am a foolish old woman. But then I was a foolish young one too. I think it was Matthew who said it; nice Matthew, who loved me just because, not needing anything, not wanting rescue, and who tried so hard, and at whom I did not look seriously for a moment. He said, "You are a fool, Madge, but a nice fool." It was probably true. And goodness, who was the other one on the stairs that first day of the reading party – *I* know who it was: Andrew Henderson – how could I have forgotten him? – who would only climb alone. *That's* who the burglar is! What was I thinking? ... I remember also looking at my grandmother's face; how that absence seemed not only absolute, but irrevocable. It is just another mystery, like everything else. Not how it is, but that it is, is the heart of things.

And Peter beside her is saying, "Gran! Gran!" trying to bring her attention back to his question. "Gran, will you mind dying?"

"I shouldn't think so, dear," she says. "It isn't our own death that troubles us. We have enough to do surviving other people's."

"Gran, you see, first we grow up and have a lot of worries. And then we die, and I don't see the point."

Heavens! the things children say! They certainly come trailing clouds of metaphysics. "It's like going on a holiday journey," she says at last. "It's not where you're going, it's what you see on the way." *When you set out for Ithaca, ask that the voyage be long . . .* what's that from? Oh, I forget so much!

The other two have melted away, back to running in the garden, hiding on the thick leafy floor of the shrubbery, climbing the lilac tree, but Peter is remorseless. "Like what things on the way, though?" he says. "Do you mean birthdays?"

"Well, yes, Peter, birthdays and other things . . . ." She smiles. Patrick, for example, lying asleep beside me in rumpled sheets, every muscle in his body slack, and on his face that shining serenity that never came to him awake. And knowing that was my doing. One can't tell such a thing to a child. . . . A piano playing in a downstairs room; Harriet in a cot beside my bed . . . a car going over the top of Exmoor; I am singing: *But not so deep as the love I'm in; I know not where I sink or swim. . . .* And something made us laugh so much we couldn't stop, and Patrick had to stop the car. I picked a handful of dark heather . . . .

"Well, we all die, but first we all live," she tells him. "Don't worry about what's the point. Just take your share. Take it two-handed and in full measure. You have to clap your hands and sing."

"Oh, yes, *I* will!" cries small Beth arriving, dancing and clapping around them. "What shall I sing?"

"Anything, anything." Madge smiles, clapping for her. We leave our mark even on our grandchildren, she thinks, small Beth more like me, Peter more like Patrick.

"And the older you get, Peter dear, the louder you must clap and sing."

"What shall we sing about?" he asks her, but his solemnity is tripping over into laughter, is getting too much for him. And, what shall we sing about? Madge asks herself. Why, whatever brute or blackguard or random chance made the world, was surely a marvellous conjuror, a dab hand at spectacle! What shall we sing about? Fish to eat fresh from the salt sea, sweet berries from the thorn, bread from the brown furrow and the orient wheat. We shall see every day, if we just raise our eyes to the hills, the movements of wind and water, and the fall of the light. There are never two moments the same, what with sky and weather, and tide, the passage of time, and the random fall of the rain. To be alive is to be bodily present, to notice where and when one is. Here we are; like amateur actors on some magnificent stage, dwarfed by the cosmic grandeur of our setting, muffing our lines, but producing now and then a fitful gleam of our own, an act of mortal beauty.

"What shall we clap?" she says to Peter. "The lifeboat in the storm. What shall we sing? O, the beauty of the world!"